專門替中國人寫的
英文課本 高級本 ▼

1片朗讀光碟
1片電腦學習光碟

李家同/策劃・審訂

文庭澍/著

暨南大學

多媒體與通訊實驗室/光碟製作

序

李家同

我一直認為我們該教英文文法的，理由很簡單，我們大多數人沒有說英文的環境，因此孩子們是不會自動說好英文的。舉例來說，很多孩子在用過去式的時候喜歡用 verb to be 的過去式，我日前看到一個孩子寫出了 "I was saw a bird"。我指出他的錯誤以後，他承認這是他很早以前所寫的，現在他已不會再犯這種錯誤了。

但是他忽然問我：「那什麼時候我們會用 was 呢？」我告訴他一個例子，"He was a teacher before." 他才恍然大悟。

我們必須承認我們中國人所犯的英文文法錯誤，都是英語母語人士不會犯的。我敢說，教育程度再差的美國孩子，也不會說出 "I was not go to school yesterday." 所以適合我們的文法書必須要針對中國人的需求來寫。

文庭澍老師寫的《專門替中國人寫的英文課本》（高級本下冊）出爐了，這本書主要的內容仍然是文法，但是文老師寫這本書採用了非常特別的方法：

(1) 她仍然將我們中國人所常犯的文法錯誤指出來了。舉例來說，我們對詞性向來大而化之，該用動詞的時候，卻常常用成名詞。我的學生就經常犯這種錯誤。

(2) 她用文章來教文法，這是完全正確的作法，看了文章以後，就更能了解文法的意義。

(3) 這本書仍然有大量的練習，有改錯，也有中翻英，這些對增進英文能力來說，都是非常有意義的。

作者自序

文庭澍

2003 和 2004 兩年的暑假，我在李家同教授指導下，一口氣寫完了《專門為中國人寫的英文課本》初、中級本一系列共四本書。這套書在當時以全英文「溝通式教學法」為主流的英文市場是個異數，但很快地便從讀者熱烈的迴響中，我們看出這套大量使用中文說明及強調文法重要性的課本有其基本需求，不但能使許多英文初學者以及在學習英文這條路上跌跌撞撞的學習者重拾信心，更能補「溝通式教學法」之不足。

寫完這四本書後，常常收到讀者來信，有些點出錯誤、有些則討論文法規則背後的理由；每次讀者來信，我必嚴肅以待，仔細回答。近年來，讀者的來信多詢問高級本何時出書，許多讀者已將初、中級本四本作業都做完了，很想循序漸進，再用高級本來繼續挑戰自己的能力。我自己對高級本已有基本構想，遲遲未動手的原因是考慮讓讀者慢慢消化四本，不必一次出齊六本，使讀者心生壓力。但近幾個月來，由於讀者和出版社不斷「施壓」，我開始認真地從讀者來信中構思高級本的明確方向。和李教授討論的結果，我們一致認為高級本不能和初、中級本一樣只有短句和會話；應以文章的型態出現，且每篇文章都應包括複雜的句型，終究日常生活中會用到的英文句型不只包含主詞、動詞和受詞而已，通常還包含許多子句及複雜的概念，一味學習簡單句型，讀者的英文能力是無法提升的。但適合讀者閱讀的文章要去哪裡找呢？整本書的主軸又該如何定位呢？

　　以我自己這幾年在大學教授大一英文、英文作文與英文新聞閱讀的經驗，發覺當今由美語班訓練而長大的學生，聽力是有些微進步，也能不怕生地開口說幾句美語，但文法觀念卻一落千丈，英文程度稍差的連《專門為中國人寫的英文課本》初級本的基本概念都不清楚，令人吃驚的是英文中上程度的學生也不知詞類變化為何物，交來的英文作業觸目皆是 "I am health."、"It is convenience."、"My interesting is playing computer games." 之類的錯誤句子。最難忘的例子是某位學生寫的下面這個句子：The food is deliciously. 當問及何以用副詞 deliciously 形容名詞 food，該生的回答居然是：「形容詞放在句尾時，不是都該加 ly 嗎？」同樣的情形還發生在一位寫了 "My happy is..." 的學生身上，當問到何以所有格代名詞 My 後面只接形容詞，該生反問：「不用形容詞要用什麼詞呢？」我搖首嘆息之餘，決定要利用高級本把各種詞類用最簡單的文字，說清楚、講明白。

　　主軸確定後，接下來該決定每一課課文以何種方法呈現？我發現一般英文課本不是以漫畫呈現課文，就是獨立的一課一文，而課文與課文之間互不相連。為了增加讀者的好奇心，我決定以連續劇的方式編寫故事，一課一段情節，情節圍繞在三個主要角色(已退休的老爸、快退休的老媽和即將考大學的兒子)的日常生活打轉。選這幾個年齡層的理由是，從讀者來信中發現其中不乏中年退休人士和年輕學子，他們也許能從主角的生活點滴中得到角色認同感。各課課文除了以情節取勝外，另有其文法的功能與目的，如希望可使讀者在閱讀課文之餘，不知不覺中了解該課所闡述的文法規則。

　　另外，為了使課文實用且生動有趣，我不斷尋找與當今社會相關的議題，如金融風暴(financial crisis)、刺激消費(boost consumption)等使讀者不但能學到各類英文字彙，還能了解社會脈動與全世界關注焦點。

　　和前四本書一樣，高級本每課先來一段導言，導言中鮮少難懂的專有名詞，而是用最簡單的話把複雜的文法概念說清楚。每一課課文都有課文解析，遇到讀者易出錯的地方，特別以「注意」標明，詳加解釋以提醒讀者。此外，每課課文後會附上大量習題，供讀者反覆演練，讀者自習的過程中如果發現自己的答案與書中的答案有出入，但不了解錯在哪裡，請寫 email 到 wentingshu@gmail.com，我一定會盡快回答。

　　這套書的完成須感謝李家同教授確立寫書的大方向，李教授雖不是我英語教學的同行，但給我的啟發，遠超過同行的大師。我的子姪們：Christian Nordin, Rachel Lin, Karen Lin, Yvonne Yeh, Miranda Lin 等人幫我潤稿；老友，也是與我合著《用英文說台灣》一書的作者 Cathy Dibell 以及負責校稿的 Chris Findler 先生提供不少寶貴的意見，最後再加上聯經出版公司何采嬪、林雅玲和陳若慈小姐的編輯專業，使這本書增色不少，當然還須加上讀者日後不斷的來信指教，定能使這套書更臻完美。

目 次

第九課 Unit 9

介系詞

互動光碟

　　介系詞是句子中的小螺絲釘,在句子中擔任的任務是連接名詞、代名詞和詞組。可別小看這些小螺絲釘,它們的功用可不小;它們可以點出某事物的空間位置,或說明某件事情是在何時、何地發生的。例如:

　　◈ The book is <u>on</u> the table.
　　　這本書在桌上。

　　◈ The book is <u>under</u> the table.
　　　這本書在桌下。

　　◈ I read the book <u>at</u> 3 o'clock <u>in</u> my room.
　　　3 點時我在我的房間讀這本書

　　◈ I read the book <u>from</u> 2:00 <u>to</u> 4:00 <u>in</u> the afternoon.
　　　我在下午的 2 點到 4 點之間讀這本書。

　　◈ <u>On</u> Monday I read the book <u>at</u> the library.
　　　星期一我在圖書館讀了這本書。

　　◈ I read the book <u>on</u> August 2nd.
　　　我八月二日讀了這本書。

　　◈ I read the book <u>during</u> 2004.
　　　2004 年時我讀了這本書。

　　◈ I read the book <u>in</u> (the) summer.
　　　夏天時我讀了這本書。

　　介系詞雖只是丁點大的螺絲釘,卻可以讓學英文的人抓狂,常常在同一個名詞,或同一類名詞的前面,使用的介系詞卻不同。請看下面一些令人困惑的介系詞用法:

◑ There are many apples <u>on</u> the tree.
樹上有許多蘋果。

◑ There are many birds <u>in</u> the tree.
樹上有許多鳥。（同樣是樹，用的介系詞卻不同。）

◑ He is <u>on</u> the bus.（<u>on</u> the motorcycle, <u>on</u> the bicycle, <u>on</u> the train, <u>on</u> the plane, <u>on</u> the ship）
他在巴士上。（上車 get <u>on</u> the bus；下車 get <u>off</u> the bus）

◑ He is <u>in</u> the car.（<u>in</u> the taxi）
他在汽車裡。（上車 get <u>in</u>（into）the car；下車 get <u>out of</u> the car）

◑ He arrived here <u>by</u> bus.（<u>by</u> car, <u>by</u> bicycle, <u>by</u> motorcycle, <u>by</u> taxi, <u>by</u> plane, <u>on</u> foot 走路）
他搭公車抵達這裡。（同樣是交通工具，用的介系詞卻有同也有異。）

◑ He went <u>to</u> bed at midnight.
他午夜 12 點上床睡覺。

◑ He lay down <u>on</u> the bed.
他躺在床上。

◑ He is <u>in</u> bed right now.
他現在正在睡覺。（同樣是床，用的介系詞卻不同。）

◑ She is standing <u>at/on</u> the corner of a street.
她正站在街角。

◑ She is hiding <u>in</u> the corner of the room.
她正躲在房間的角落裡。（同樣是 corner，用的介系詞就不同。）

⑨ We watched a movie <u>in</u> the theater.
我們在電影院看電影。

⑨ We watched a movie <u>on</u> television.
我們看電視上播放的電影。(同樣是看電影,用的介系詞卻不同。)

⑨ <u>At the end</u> of the movie, we all laughed.
電影結尾時,我們都笑了。

⑨ <u>In the end</u>, I decided to leave this place for good.
最後,我決定永遠離開此地。(同樣形容 the end,介系詞卻不同。)

＊ 注意:for good(永遠)。

從上面例子看來,介系詞實在不容易,不過如果能歸納出一個系統,也許比較容易入門:

I. 標明地方的介系詞:

最常用的介系詞:in, at, on

1. in:

in the room(在房間裡)、in the store(在店裡)、in the car(在車裡)、in the taxi(在計程車裡)、in the water(在水裡)、in the ocean(在海裡)、in the living room(在客廳裡)、in the park(在公園裡)、in the city(在城市裡,如 in Taidong 在台東)、in the country(在鄉間;在該國,如 in Taiwan 在台灣)、in the world(在世界上)、in southern Taiwan(在台灣南部)、in the yard(在院子裡)、in the pool(在游泳池裡)、in the sky(在天空上)、in the picture(在圖片裡)、in the book(在書裡)、in the newspaper(在報上)、in the diary(在日記裡)

2. at:

　　at home(在家)、at work(在工作)、at the station(在車站)、at the bus stop(在公車站牌)、at the traffic light(紅綠燈前)、at the desk(在書桌前)、at the airport(在機場)、at the supermarket(在超市)、at a party(在派對上)、at a basketball game(在籃球比賽)、at the concert(在音樂會上)、at the post office(在郵局)

3. on:

　　on the 10th floor(在十樓)、on the floor(在地上)、on the bike/bicyde(在腳踏車上)、on the motorcycle(在摩托車上)、on the bus(在公車上)、on the train(在火車上)、on a plane(在飛機上)、on a boat(在小船上)、on a ship(在大船上)、on the street(在街上)、on the balcony(在陽台上)、on the wall(在牆上)、on page 39(在 39 頁上)、on TV(電視上)、on the phone(在講電話)、on campus(在校園裡)

　　現以句子為例，說明標明地方的介系詞用法：

　　§ There is a light <u>above/over</u> my head.
　　　我的頭上有一盞燈。

　　§ The box is <u>below/under</u> the sink.
　　　盒子在洗臉槽的下方。

　　§ He is sitting <u>between</u> his mom and dad.
　　　他正坐在他爸爸和媽媽的中間。

　　§ <u>Among</u> all the students, she is the tallest.
　　　所有學生中她最高。

　　§ <u>Beside/Next to</u> the cat, there is a puppy.
　　　在貓的旁邊有隻小狗。

🔊 In front of me, I found a red envelope.

我在我的前面發現一個紅包。

🔊 I can't discover anyone behind/in back of me.

我沒辦法發現身後有沒有人。

🔊 She likes to sit in the front/back/middle of the classroom.

她喜歡坐在教室的前面/後面/中央。

🔊 In the picture, she is on the right/on the left.

照片中，她在右邊/左邊。

🔊 She likes to sit next to/beside/by the window.

她喜歡坐在窗邊。

🔊 There is a drug store across from the school.

學校的對面有間藥房。

🔊 She often takes walks with him.

她常跟他一起散步。

🔊 He is sitting at the table/at the computer.

他正坐在桌前/電腦前。

🔊 He sits on the chair.

他坐在椅子上。

🔊 He lives near the convenience store.

他住在便利商店附近。

II. 標明時間的介系詞：

1. 時刻

🔊 I woke up at 8:00 this morning.

我今天早上八點起床。

🔊 I surfed the Internet <u>from</u> 8:00 <u>to</u> 10:00 this morning.

今天早上我從 8 點上網到 10 點。

🔊 I surfed the Internet <u>for</u> four hours.

我上網長達 4 小時。

🔊 I will be there <u>in</u> 10 minutes.

我 10 分鐘內趕到。

🔊 You have to be in class <u>on</u> time.

你得準時來上課。

🔊 I arrived at the theater just <u>in</u> time for the show.

我及時趕到劇院看秀。

🔊 I have to be in class <u>by</u> 8:10 in the morning.

我早上必須不晚於 8 點 10 分到教室。

🔊 I have to be in class <u>before</u> 8:10 in the morning.

我必須在早上 8 點 10 分以前到教室。

＊ 注意：before 8:10 是指 8:10 以前一定要到，8:10 到都不行。

　　by 8:10 則只要不晚於 8:10 都可以。

2. 上午、中午、下午、晚上

🔊 I met her <u>in</u> the morning.

我早上跟她見了面。

🔊 I went to the bank <u>at</u> noon.

我中午去了銀行。

🔊 I took a nap <u>in</u> the afternoon.

我下午睡了午覺。

🔊 I watched TV <u>in</u> the evening.

我晚上看了電視。

🎧　I checked my e-mail <u>at</u> night.
　　我晚上檢查有沒有電子郵件。

🎧　I often sleep late <u>on</u> Sunday morning.
　　星期天早上我常晚起。

🎧　I didn't do anything <u>this</u> morning.
　　今早我什麼事都沒做。

🎧　I missed the last train <u>last</u> night.
　　昨晚我沒趕上最後一班火車。

　　＊注意：last, this 前面都不用加介系詞。

3. 星期

🎧　We will meet <u>on</u> Friday.
　　我們星期五會見面。

🎧　<u>On</u> weekends, we usually buy some groceries.
　　週末我們通常會去買菜。

🎧　We had a meeting <u>this</u> Thursday.
　　這星期四我們開了一個會。

🎧　We will have a meeting <u>next</u> Wednesday.
　　下星期三我們要開會。

　　＊注意：this, next 前面都不用加介系詞。

例外：

🎧　<u>Since</u> <u>last</u> Wednesday, I have been a vegetarian.
　　我從上星期三開始吃素。

4. 日期

🔊 I was born <u>on</u> November 8th, 1978.
我生於 1978 年 11 月 8 日。

🔊 <u>On</u> the 2nd of January, I will be in Brazil.
1 月 2 日我會在巴西。

🔊 <u>On</u> my birthday, I don't usually eat cake.
我生日時通常不吃蛋糕。

5. 月份

🔊 I was born <u>in</u> May.
我是在 5 月出生的。

🔊 They got married <u>last</u> July.
他們去年 7 月結婚了。

🔊 We are getting married <u>this</u> September.
我們今年 9 月要結婚。

　　＊ 注意：last, this 前面都不用加介系詞。

例外：

🔊 <u>Since</u> <u>this</u> August, I have been writing my blog.
今年 8 月起我開始寫我的部落格。

6. 年份

🔊 She was born <u>in</u> 1952.
她是在 1952 年出生的。

🔊 <u>During</u> 1983 I lived in Taoyuan.
1983 年間我住在桃園。

℗ I have been living in Taichung <u>since</u> 1978.
自從 1978 年起我一直住在台中。

℗ <u>From</u> 1970 <u>to</u> 2007, I moved 5 times.
從 1970 年到 2007 年我搬了 5 次家。

℗ <u>In</u> the 1970s, many college graduates studied abroad.
70 年代許多大學畢業生出國留學。

7. 世紀

℗ In the 21st century, teachers have to face new challenges.
21 世紀老師必須面對新的挑戰。

8. 季節

℗ I will visit my cousins <u>in</u>(the) fall.
秋天我會去看表兄弟姊妹。

℗ I visited my aunt <u>this</u> summer.
今年夏天我去看了阿姨。

℗ I got my driver's license <u>last</u> winter.
去年冬天我拿到了駕駛執照。

＊ 注意：last, this 前面都不用加介系詞。

例外：

℗ <u>Since</u> <u>last</u> spring, I have been waiting for him to show up.
去年春天起，我一直在等他出現。

℗ If he can't finish <u>by</u> <u>next</u> fall, I will ask someone else to do the job.
如果明年秋天他還無法完成，我會叫別人做這份工作。

9. 節慶

℗ at Christmas 聖誕節期間

on Christmas Eve 聖誕夜
on New Year's Day 新年
on Chinese New Year's Eve 除夕
on the Dragon Boat Festival 端午節
on the Moon Festival 中秋節
on the Lantern Festival 元宵節
on Tomb Sweeping Day 清明節
on Teacher's Day 教師節
on Double Tenth Day 國慶日
on April Fool's Day 愚人節
on Valentine's Day 情人節

＊注意：on 可以用 during 取代。

III. 常用的形容詞與介系詞：

be interested in 對……感到有趣
They are interested in reading books.
他們對閱讀書籍感興趣。

be tired of 對……感到疲倦、厭倦……
We are tired of watching TV.
我們看膩電視了。

be worried about 對……感到憂心
They are worried about their future.
他們對自己的未來感到憂心。

be satisfied with 對……感到滿意
They are satisfied with the results.
他們對結果感到滿意。

be shocked by 對……感到吃驚

🔊　We are shocked by the news.
　　我們對那則新聞感到震驚。

be afraid of 對……感到害怕

🔊　They are afraid of dogs.
　　他們怕狗。

be jealous of 對……嫉妒

🔊　They are jealous of her success.
　　他們嫉妒她的成功。

be familiar with 對……熟悉

🔊　We are familiar with those books.
　　我們熟悉這些書。

be fond of 對……喜歡

🔊　They are fond of sports.
　　他們喜歡運動。

be proud of 對……感到驕傲、以……為榮

🔊　She is proud of her children.
　　她以她的孩子為榮。

IV. 常用的介系詞片語（介系詞＋名詞）：

on: on purpose（故意地）、on sale（出售中）、on trial（受審判中）、on duty（值勤中）、on holiday（英式）／on vacation（美式）（度假中）、on strike（罷工中）、on fire（起火了）

in: in trouble（有麻煩）、in tears（流淚）、in love（戀愛中）、in power（執政中）、in debt（負債中）、in danger（處於危險中）、in my opinion（以我的意見看來）、in red（穿著紅色衣物）

at: at ease(放鬆、安心)、at work(在工作)、at home(在家)、at the first try(第一次嘗試)

out of: out of control(無法控制的)、out of date(過時)、out of order(故障)、out of fashion(退流行)

by: by accident(無意中)、by mistake(無意中、不小心)、by luck(僥倖地)

for: for a while(一會兒)、for the first time(第一次)

V. 動詞與介系詞的組合，如：look at, show up, check in... 屬動詞片語，請看高級本上冊第四課。

朗讀 CD 第 1 軌

互動光碟

9-1 生字 Vocabulary

ball game	(n.)球賽
leave for	(ph.)離開;前往……;動身去……
except for	(ph.)除了……之外沒有
suggest	(v.)建議
shaved ice	(n.)剉冰
steps	(n.)腳步
sweaty and smelly	(adj.)臭汗淋漓
agree with	(ph.)同意(人)
oldest child	(n.)長子(女)
middle child	(n.)(中間的小孩)次子(女)
opinion	(n.)意見
follow	(v.)跟從(follow, followed, followed)
envy	(v.)羨慕(envy, envied, envied)
only child	(n.)獨生子女
feel pressured	(ph.)覺得有壓力
anxiously	(adv.)焦慮地

n.＝名詞　ph.＝詞組　v.＝動詞　adv.＝副詞　adj.＝形容詞

balcony	(n.)陽台
in vain	(ph.)沒有用、徒勞
blog	(n.)部落格
exactly	(adv.)正好

朗讀 CD 第 2 軌

互動光碟

9-2 課文 Text

After the **ball game**, all of our friends **left for** home **except for**[1] Jie Ming, Hong Sheng, and me. Jie Ming **suggested**[2] we go to the coffee shop at the corner of the street, but I thought we should have **shaved ice**[3] at the roadside stand a few **steps** from the school instead. Since we were **sweaty and smelly**[4], I thought it would be better for us to eat and drink outside. They all **agreed with**[5] me.

Jie Ming is the **oldest**[6] **child** in his family. He likes to be in charge of[7] things. Unlike Jie Ming, Hong Sheng is a **middle child**. He is not used to[8] giving any **opinions**; he just **follows**. They both **envy** me because I am an **only child**. But what they don't know is that I often **feel** lonely and **pressured**[9].

When I got home, my parents were **anxiously**[10] waiting for me at the door. "Inky disappeared!" Mom cried, "Inky is not under the bookshelves; nor[11] is he hiding behind the door." Dad added, "I looked for him everywhere on the **balcony**, but **in vain**!" In the evening, I wrote on my **blog**: "On July 31st, at **exactly** 10 o'clock in the morning, we lost Inky. I really hope Inky will show up tomorrow."

9-3 課文翻譯

　　球賽結束後，除了傑明、宏生和我之外，所有朋友都回家了。傑明提議我們去街角的咖啡店，但我覺得我們應該去離學校不到幾步的路邊攤去吃剉冰，既然我們滿身臭汗，我覺得還是在外面吃喝比較好。他們都同意我的提議。

　　傑明是家中的長子，他喜歡掌控事情。跟傑明不同，宏生排行老二，他不習慣出意見，只是跟著他人的腳步走。他們都很羨慕我，因為我是獨生子，可是他們不知道我常覺得寂寞、有壓力。

　　我到家時，爸媽正焦急地等在門口。媽媽大聲說：「小墨不見了！牠不在書架底下，也沒躲在門後面。」爸爸加了一句：「我找遍了陽台也沒找到！」當天晚上，我在部落格裡寫著：「7月 31 日，早上 10 點整，小墨走失了。我真希望小墨明天就會出現。」

9-4 解析 Language Focus

互動光碟

1.　except, except for 和 besides 很容易混用，except 和 except for 是指「除了……之外」，如：

🎧 I ate everything on the plate <u>except</u> (<u>except for</u>) the eggplant.
　　除了茄子之外，盤子裡什麼我都吃了。

🎧 <u>Except for</u> her, we will be there on time.
　　除了她以外，我們都會準時到那裡。
　　＊注意：後面接 her (受詞)而不是 she。

🎧 This winter vacation was nice <u>except</u> that it was a bit cold.
　　今年寒假除了冷了一點外，其他都很好。

🎧 She made no comment <u>except</u> to point out a typo.
　　她除了指出一個拼錯的字，沒有給任何評語。

　　從上面的例子可看出 except for 後面只能接名詞，而 except 可以接名詞、介系詞片語或句子，不過因為口語的影響，except for 和 except 漸漸可以互換使用，例如下面的句子，except for 後面也可以接句子和介系詞，但以 that 開頭的子句和不定詞(to＋v)，前面還是只能用 except。另外，except for 表「如果不是……」或放在句首時，不能以 except 取代。

🎧 She is quite nice <u>except</u> (<u>for</u>) when she is angry.
　　她人很和氣，生氣的時候除外。

🎧 I can sleep almost anywhere <u>except</u> (<u>for</u>) on a plane.
　　除了在飛機上之外，我哪兒都能睡。

besides＝in addition to 除了……外還有

🎧 <u>Besides</u> coffee, we also serve tea.
　　除了咖啡外，我們還供應茶。

例 Besides English, we have to study Japanese.
除了英文外，我們還得學日文。

beside＝next to 在……的旁邊

例 She is sitting beside the big guy.
她正坐在一個大塊頭的旁邊。

2. suggest 建議、propose 提議、recommend 推薦、insist 堅持、demand 要求，這幾個動詞的用法很特殊，請看下面例句：

例 I suggested（that）she（should）take a break.
我建議她休息一下。

例 I suggested（that）she（should）not go to work for a few days.
我建議她幾天不要去上班。

例 I insisted（that）something（should）be done.
我堅持要做件事。

＊注意：錯誤的句型，請看如何改正：

例 I suggested ~~her to~~ she take a shower first.
我建議她先沖個澡。

例 I demanded he ~~goes~~ to work right now.
我要求他現在去上班。

例 I recommended ~~her not to~~ she not stay up late.
我建議她不要熬夜。

3. shave（動詞三態 shave, shaved, shaved），shaved ice 的意思是剉冰，因為冰是要被剉的，故以動詞第三態變化（過去分詞）表示之。

4. sweat 汗（名詞）、sweaty 出汗的（形容詞），如：a sweaty hand 多汗的手；smell 氣味（名詞）、smelly 臭的（形容詞），如：a smelly room 有臭味的房間

5. agree with（a person 人, an opinion 意見, a policy 政策）；agree on（a decision 決定, a date 日期）；agree to（do something 做某件事情, a suggestion 建議）

6. old, 比較級 older... than, 最高級 the oldest

7. be in charge(of) 負責

   𝄞 Who is in charge?
   誰是老大？誰主事？

   charge 還有其他用法

   be free of charge 免費

   to charge a battery 充電(池)

8. be(get) used to＋動詞 ing 習慣於

   𝄞 I am used to brushing my teeth after meals.
   我習慣於飯後刷牙。

   used to＋動詞原形　過去經常做……

   𝄞 I didn't use to brush my teeth after meals, but now I do.
   我過去飯後都不刷牙，現在會刷了。

9. pressure 壓力(名詞)，pressured 感到有壓力的(形容詞)

   𝄞 I am under a lot of pressure.
   我承受很大的壓力。

   𝄞 They put a lot of pressure on her.
   他們給她很大的壓力。

   𝄞 High blood pressure runs in my family.
   我家人都有高血壓的毛病。

   𝄞 I often feel pressured before tests.
   考試前我常常覺得有壓力。

10. anxious 擔心(形容詞)，anxiously 憂慮地(副詞)，anxiety 憂慮(名詞)

    𝄞 We are getting anxious about money.
    我們開始擔心錢的問題。

✿ They are <u>anxiously</u> watching the news on TV.

我們焦慮地看著電視新聞。

✿ His voice is full of <u>anxiety</u>.

他的聲音充滿焦慮。

11. 同時介紹兩個否定句時可以用 nor 或 neither 來連接。如：

✿ I don't like steak, <u>nor</u> do I like sushi.

我不喜歡吃牛排，也不喜歡吃壽司。

✿ I can't ride a scooter, <u>nor</u> can I drive a car.

我不會騎機車，也不會開車。

✿ I am not outgoing, <u>nor</u> am I shy.

我不外向，也不害羞。

9-5-1選選看

1. In order to catch the Taiwan High Speed Rail, I have to leave _____ 3:30 P.M.
   (a) in   (b) by   (c) on

2. I parked my car_____ a green SUV(休旅車) and a blue van(箱型車).
   (a) at   (b) besides   (c) between

3. Look at the woman _____ the picture. Who is she?
   (a) in   (b) on   (c) at

4. I don't agree _____ you. _____ my opinion, you're wrong.
   (a) to, For   (b) with, In   (c) on, In

5. She plays tennis _____ Sunday.
   (a) on   (b) at   (c) for

6. We have been waiting for her _____ seven o'clock.
   (a) for   (b) at   (c) since

7. The house is _____ sale right now.
   (a) in   (b) on   (c) for

8. I have to finish this essay _____ Tuesday.
   (a) by   (b) in   (c) since

9. He put salt in his coffee _____ mistake.
   (a) on   (b) for   (c) by

10. What do you usually do _____ the weekend?
    (a) with   (b) on   (c) in

11. The news you told me is _____ date. In fact, their lives are back to normal now.

    (a) out of　(b) on　(c) from

12. The movie lasts _____ 2 hours and 15 minutes.

    (a) at　(b) for　(c) in

13. I must go back home _____ the movie. I have to be home _____ 8 o'clock.

    (a) to, at　(b) to, after　(c) after, by

14. When the bus stops, she gets _____ the bus.

    (a) out　(b) off　(c) of

15. I spoke to him _____ the phone.

    (a) for　(b) on　(c) with

16. He came here _____ bicycle.

    (a) on　(b) with　(c) by

17. There were no computers _____ the 19th century.

    (a) in　(b) on　(c) at

18. I am not familiar _____ the book.

    (a) to　(b) in　(c) with

19. I had a terrible headache, so I didn't go to work _____ last Friday.

    (a) on　(b) X　(c) for

20. He is_____ ease on the sofa with his father's arm around him.

    (a) at　(b) on　(c) with

21. Please wait a second. I will be there _____ a minute.

    (a) in　(b) for　(c) at

22. _____the moment, I don't have a job.

    (a) In　(b) On　(c) At

23. I will start my new job _____ next October.

    (a) on　(b) in　(c) X

24. I found his secrets _____ accident.

　　(a) in　(b) on　(c) by

25. You can buy stamps _____ the post office_____ Wanfang Street.

　　(a) on, at　(b) at, on　(c) in, at

9-5-2 填填看（＊注意：句子第一個字母要用大寫。）

on,　at,　from,　since,　for,　in,　X

1. _____1990 to 2000, I lived in Pingtong.

2. I am not going anywhere _____ spring.

3. _____ a few days I will be in Beijing.

4. This Russian movie（俄國片） was shown here _____ the first time.

5. I have never gone hiking _____ November 8th.

6. I was very sleepy _____ midnight.

7. I won't go anywhere _____ next Tuesday.

8. We eat fish _____ New Year's Eve（除夕）.

9. We eat rice dumplings _____ the Dragon Boat Festival.

10. Many schools have a long break _____ spring.

on,　at,　from,　for,　in

11. My girlfriend is the person _____ the right _____ the picture.

12. The girl always hides _____ the corner of the classroom.

13. Don't always sit _____ the computer.

14. I found some old photos _____ the drawer（抽屜） of my dad's desk.

15. He got _____ a taxi and headed quickly for the airport.

16. She has been talking with her boyfriend _____ the phone _____ two hours.

17. I live _____ the second floor of my building.

18. The person who lives across_____ our house is an engineer.

19. _____the corner of the street, you will find a gym.

20. The teacher asked us to do the exercises _____ page 103.

in, of, with, about, by

21. I am not satisfied _____ the service at the convenience store.
22. She is really fond _____ teaching little kids.
23. They are proud _____ their children.
24. If you don't agree _____ him, you have to speak up.
25. I am not familiar _____ this new book.
26. The book is full _____ mistakes.
27. Some classmates are really jealous _____ her.
28. We are tired _____ singing this song again and again.
29. She is very anxious _____ the unfinished work.
30. Her room was _____ a mess.

in, at, out of, on, by

31. After the typhoon, many home phones were _____ order.
32. I can't chat with you right now. I am _____ duty.
33. When Ms. Lin left our school, many of her students were _____ tears.
34. We are on the same bus _____ chance.
35. I don't answer the phone when I am _____ holiday.
36. I passed the exam _____ the first try.
37. She fell on the floor _____ purpose in order to attract his attention.
38. He always dresses _____ green because he belongs to the Green Party.
39. _____ short, this is the lesson we should all learn.
40. They have been _____ love for almost 10 years.

9-5-3問答

1. After the ball game, who went back home right away?

   _____

2. Where did Jie Ming suggest they have a drink?（He suggested）

   _____

3. What did the writer think about Jie Ming's suggestion?（He thought they should）

   _____

4. Why it was better for them to eat and drink outside?

   _____

5. Among Jie Ming, Hong Sheng, and the writer, who likes to be in charge of things?

   _____

6. What does the writer think about being an only child in his family?

   _____

7. Who is not used to giving opinions?

   _____

8. Why were the writer's parents anxiously waiting for him?

   _____

9. Was Inky on the balcony?

   _____

10. At what time did Inky disappear?

   _____

9-5-4改錯

1. Who will be charge this meeting?

2. Inky was disappeared yesterday.

3. She suggested us to drink some coffee first.

4. On summer we usually go to the beach.

5. There is a drug store a few steps to the school.

6. Who told you that we jealous you?

7. She grew lots of plants at the balcony.

8. I will show up in front of your house at ten minutes.

9. My summer vacation lasts in two months.

10. I afraid of cockroaches（蟑螂）.

11. In my way to school, I stopped at a roadside stand.

12. He is not used to eat at roadside stands.

9-5-5英文該怎麼寫？

1. 這個電腦遊戲已經過時了。

_____

2. 我們滿意今晚的籃球賽。

_____

3. 媽媽建議我先去做功課（do my homework first）。

_____

4. 我是家中的老大，但是他是家中的老么。

_____

5. 我桌上的書不見了。（The books...）

_____

6. 他不吃也不喝。（He didn't..., nor...）

_____

7. 以我的意見，小墨一定正躲在陽台上。（In my opinion, ...）

_____

8.　我不習慣半夜以前上床。(I am not used to...)

　　_____

9.　他們只是羨慕你，不是嫉妒你。

　　_____

10.　他到處找遺失的鑰匙卻徒勞無功(in vain)。

　　_____

第十課 Unit 10

連接詞

互動光碟

連接詞與介系詞一樣，像個小螺絲釘，在句子中擔任的角色是連接字、詞和句。例如：

🎧 I talked to Mom <u>and</u> Dad on the phone.
我跟爸媽講電話。(連接詞 and 連接 Mom 和 Dad 兩個字。)

🎧 I can't decide <u>whether</u> to go to medical school <u>or</u> to go to law school.
我無法決定要讀醫學院還是法學院。(whether... or... 這一對連接詞連接 to go to medical school 和 to go to law school 兩個詞。)

🎧 You can call me <u>when</u> you are ready.
你準備好了可以打電話給我。(連接詞 when 連接 You can call me.和 You are ready.兩個句子。)

連接詞可以簡單分為三大類：對等連接詞、從屬連接詞和相關連接詞。現在分別介紹這三大類連接詞，並用例句說明它們各自的用法：

I. 對等連接詞

它有個好玩的名字叫做 fanboys，因為對等連接詞包括 <u>f</u>or, <u>a</u>nd, <u>n</u>or, <u>b</u>ut, <u>o</u>r, <u>y</u>et, <u>s</u>o，每個字的第一個字母合起來正好是 fanboys。對等連接詞連接字、詞和句子，其中 but 和 for 除了當連接詞外，還可以當作介系詞。

🎧 I often take the Taiwan High Speed Rail, <u>for</u> it only takes me one hour to get to Kaohsiung.
我常搭高鐵，因為只花我 1 小時就可以到高雄。

🎧 Jackie Chan <u>and</u> Jet Li are my two favorite action movie stars.
成龍和李連杰是我最喜歡的動作片明星。

He sent a voicemail to her <u>and</u> waited by the phone for an answer.
他留言給她，接著在電話旁等她的回音。

He doesn't use a cell phone, <u>nor</u> does he surf the Internet.
他不用手機，也不上網。

I won't go to his birthday party, <u>but</u> I will give him a gift.
我不會去他的生日派對，但我會送他禮物。

You can order fried noodles <u>or</u> fried rice.
你可以點炒麵或炒飯。

She spent hours teaching me, <u>yet</u> I still don't understand.
她花好幾個小時教我，但我還是不懂。

She often goes to bed early, <u>so</u> you had better call her now.
她通常早睡，所以你最好現在打給她。

II. 從屬連接詞

從屬連接詞連接一個主要句子和它的附屬句子。常用的從屬連接詞如下：

<u>After</u> he graduated from school, he quickly found a high-paying job.（此句中主要句子是 He quickly found a high-paying job. 它的附屬句子是 he graduated from school.）
他畢業後很快找到了一份高薪工作。

<u>Although</u> I've never studied French, I can guess the meaning of some words.
雖然我從沒學過法文，但我可以猜出某些字的意思。
＊注意：使用 although 的句型，but 不必寫出。

<u>As</u> you can see, we are very busy.
如你所見，我們非常忙。

互動光碟

◎ She kissed her cat <u>as if/as though</u> it were her baby.
她親她的貓咪，好似牠是她的小嬰兒。
＊注意：貓不是她的 baby，假設語氣中 be 動詞用 were 而非 was。

◎ <u>As long as</u> you hand in your homework on time, I won't fail you.
只要你準時交作業，我就不會當你。

◎ She didn't come to class <u>because</u> her mom was ill.
她沒有來上課，因為她母親生病了。

◎ <u>Before</u> meeting the writer, I didn't know she was your aunt.
見這位作家之前，我不知道她是你的阿姨。

◎ He felt jealous of his wife's success <u>even though</u> he knew he shouldn't.
他嫉妒他太太的成就，即使他知道自己不該如此。

◎ <u>If</u> you invite her, she will come.
如果你約她的話，她一定會來。

◎ <u>If only</u> you knew the title of the book, I would give it to you.
只要你知道書名，我就把書送給你。

◎ <u>In order to</u> attract more students, the library bought some comic books.
為了吸引更多的學生，圖書館添購了一些漫畫書。

◎ <u>Once</u> she makes a decision, she never changes her mind.
一旦她作了決定，她絕不會改變心意。

◎ I like to see movies in the theater <u>rather than</u> watch DVDs at home.
我喜歡去電影院看電影，而不喜歡在家看 DVD。

◎ <u>Since</u> you came early, you could help us set the table.

既然你來得早，你可以幫我們擺碗筷。

🎧 He arrived early <u>so that</u> he would get a seat in the front row.
他來得早，為的是可以坐前排的位子。

🎧 <u>Unless</u> I get an extra ticket, I don't have one to give to you.
除非我多拿到一張票，否則我沒有票可以給你。

🎧 <u>When</u> I walked into the kitchen, I saw a mouse under the fridge.
我走進廚房時，看到冰箱下面有一隻老鼠。

🎧 <u>Whenever</u> I brush my teeth, my gums bleed.
我每次刷牙時，牙齦都出血。

🎧 <u>Wherever</u> she goes, he follows.
她去哪兒，他就跟到哪兒。

🎧 She likes name-brand products; <u>whereas</u> her sister likes pirated ones.
她喜歡名牌，可是她的姊姊喜歡仿冒品。

🎧 <u>While</u> I was taking a shower, he called.
當我正在沖澡時，他來電了。

III. 相關連接詞

相關連接詞總是成對出現，通常我們用這種成對的連接詞來銜接句子中相同詞性的兩個詞(如連結兩個名詞或兩個形容詞)。常用的相關連接詞有 both... and, either...or, neither... nor, not only... but also, so... as, whether... or。現在用例句說明它們的用法：

🎧 <u>Both</u> Peter <u>and</u> John work in the same restaurant.
彼得和約翰都在同一家餐館工作。

🎧 Could you order <u>either</u> a chicken sandwich <u>or</u> a hamburger for me?

互動光碟

你可以幫我點雞肉三明治或漢堡嗎?

🦻 I am <u>neither</u> hungry <u>nor</u> thirsty.
我既不餓也不渴。

🦻 She can't decide <u>whether</u> to go to a business school <u>or</u> to go to a law school.
她決定不了要進商學院還是法學院。

🦻 He is <u>not only</u> her husband <u>but also</u> her co-worker.
他不但是她的先生,也是她的同事。

🦻 This dress isn't <u>so</u> pretty <u>as</u> that one.
這件洋裝不像那一件那麼漂亮。

朗讀 CD 第 4 軌

互動光碟

10-1 生字 Vocabulary

dream of	(ph.)夢到
icon	(n.)圖像、偶像
be curious about	(ph.)好奇
surprise	(n.)吃驚
striped	(adj.)條紋的
furious	(adj.)生氣的
firmly	(adv.)堅決地
debate	(v.)盤算(debate, debated, debated)
upset	(adj.)懊惱的
digital camera	(n.)數位相機
post	(v.)貼在(網站上)(post, posted, posted)
adopt	(v.)領養(adopt, adopted, adopted)
receive	(v.)收到(receive, received, received)
local	(adj.)本地的
abroad	(n.)國外
Iran	(n.)伊朗

n.＝名詞　ph.＝詞組　v.＝動詞　adv.＝副詞　adj.＝形容詞

Brazil	(n.)巴西
South Africa	(n.)南非
applicant	(n.)申請者
single mother	(n.)單親媽媽
sincere	(adj.)誠懇的

朗讀 CD 第 5 軌

互動光碟

10-2 課文 Text

I don't usually have dreams, but last night I **dreamed of** my cat, Inky. In my dream, a pink Hello Kitty, the Japanese comic **icon**[1], was trying to make friends with our Inky. Inky looked afraid, yet[2] he **was curious about** Hello Kitty. The sound of a cat suddenly woke me up. To my **surprise**[3], Inky was standing right in front of me. On his right, there was a **striped**[4] and fluffy cute little kitten that was not Hello Kitty.

"Come and look! Not only[5] did Inky come back, but he also brought back a kitten." Dad looked **furious**. He said **firmly**[6], "One is enough." Mom seemed to be **debating**[7] whether we could keep two cats or not. I thought they would be happy to see Inky back, but both Mom and Dad looked rather **upset**[8].

I quickly jumped out of my bed and took out my **digital camera**. After taking some pictures[9] of the kitten, I **posted**[10] them on the Internet, hoping someone would **adopt** her. A few days later, I **received** some messages, both **local** and from **abroad**. Some were from as far as **Iran**, **Brazil**, and **South Africa**. One **applicant**[11], a **single mother**, sounded **sincere** and seemed to like cats, and so did[12] another 30-year-old man. I decided to interview them both first, then make a decision.

10-3 課文翻譯

我通常不太作夢，但是昨晚我卻夢到了我的貓小墨。在夢裡，日本漫畫人物──粉紅色的 Hello Kitty 要跟我們的小墨作朋友，小墨看起來怕怕的，但還是對 Hello Kitty 充滿好奇。突然有隻貓的聲音把我吵醒了。讓我驚訝的是，小墨居然站在我的正前方，他的右方有隻身上有條紋、毛茸茸的可愛小貓，牠可不是 Hello Kitty。

「來看啊！小墨不只回來了，他還帶回一隻小貓。」爸看起來很生氣，他堅定地說：「養一隻就夠了。」媽媽似乎在考慮要不要留下兩隻貓。我以為他們看到小墨回來會覺得高興，但他們兩個看起來相當苦惱。

我很快跳下床，拿出我的數位相機，幫小貓照了幾張照片後，登在網路上，希望有人來認養牠。幾天後，我收到了來自國內外的回音，有的甚至遠從伊朗、巴西和南非寫信來。其中有位單親媽媽申請人聽起來很誠懇，也似乎蠻愛貓的，還有一位 30 歲的男士聽起來也一樣誠懇。我決定先跟他們兩位面談，再做決定。

朗讀 CD 第 6 軌

 互動光碟

 10-4 解析 Language Focus

1. icon 電腦上的圖像，comic icon 是指具有代表性的漫畫人物

2. yet 與對等連接詞 but 的用法一樣

　⑨ I don't eat much, yet I am over 60 kg.
　　我吃得不多，但還是超過 60 公斤。

3. (much) to one's surprise 令某人(大為)吃驚的是(介系詞 to＋所有格 my＋表示情緒的名詞 surprise)

　⑨ To my surprise, he decided to accept my invitation.
　　令我吃驚的是，他居然決定接受我的邀約。

to his delight 令他高興的是……

　⑨ To his delight, he won first prize.
　　令他高興的是，他居然得到頭獎。

to our amusement 令我們覺得有趣的是……

　⑨ To our amusement, she sprayed him with water.
　　令我們覺得有趣的是，她居然把水噴在他身上。

to their disappointment 令他們失望的是……

　⑨ To their disappointment, she didn't show up as she had promised.
　　令他們失望的是，她居然沒有依約出現。

to her annoyance 令她不快的是……

　⑨ To her annoyance, her son failed half of his courses.
　　令她惱火的是，她的兒子居然有一半課程沒過。

4. striped 有條紋的，如 striped shirt 條紋襯衫。襯衫樣式還有其他說法：

9 plaid shirt
格子襯衫

9 polka dot shirt
圓點襯衫

9 patterned shirt
花襯衫

5. not only... but also 不僅……而且……，not only 置於句首時要用倒裝句

9 Not only can I speak English, but I can also speak Japanese.
我不僅會說英文，還會說日文。

6. firm 堅定的、堅決的(形容詞)，firmly 堅決地、堅定地(副詞)

9 He is a firm Christian.
他是很虔誠的基督徒。

9 He rejected her offer firmly.
他堅決拒絕她的報價。

7. debate 辯論、爭議、考慮

9 They are debating who should be the winner.
他們在爭論誰才是贏家。

9 He is debating whether to stay or leave.
他在考慮要留下或離開。

8. upset 使煩亂(動詞三態 upset, upset, upset)

9 The bad result upset me.
不好的結果讓我心煩。

9 I was upset by their unfriendly criticism.
我對他們不友好的批評感到心煩。

upset stomach 腸胃不適

🄰 Because he had an upset stomach, he went home early.
因為腸胃不適，所以他早早回家了。

9. take pictures（photos） 照相

🄰 He likes to take pictures of his cat.
他喜歡幫他的貓照相。

10. post 貼上（動詞），流行網路用字

11. apply 申請（動詞）、application 申請書（名詞）、applicant 申請者（名詞）

🄰 He is applying for a work permit.
他正在申請工作證。

🄰 Before applying for the job, you need to fill out an application form.
申請工作之前，你得先填申請表。

🄰 Many applicants fail to meet our requirements.
許多應徵者不符合我們的條件。

12. 口語常用 me too 或 me neither 表示自己跟別人想法一樣，如：

🄰 A: I am hungry. 我很餓。

B: Me too. 我也很餓。

＝A: I am hungry.

B: So am I.（I am hungry, and so is he.）

A: I am not hungry. 我不餓。

B: Me neither. 我也不餓。

＝A: I am not hungry.

B: Neither am I.（I am not hungry, and neither is he.）

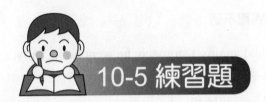

10-5 練習題

10-5-1 選選看

1. She has a cat _____ a rabbit.
    (a) nor   (b) and   (c) but

2. He opened the door_____ walked into the building
    (a) so   (b) yet   (c) and

3. Our flag is red, white, _____ blue.
    (a) besides   (b) and   (c) but

4. It began to rain, _____ I put on my raincoat.
    (a) but   (b) or   (c) so

5. Mr. Hu doesn't wear ties, _____ Mr. Huang does.
    (a) and   (b) but   (c) or

6. A: I don't like hamburgers.
   B: I don't _____.
    (a) Nor   (b) Either   (c) Neither

7. A: I am tired.
   B: _____ am I.
    (a) so   (b) either   (c) neither

8. _____ I had a headache, I went to work.
    (a) Because   (b) Even though   (c) When

9. I'll be there at 3:00, _____ will Amy.
    (a) but   (b) so   (c) nor

10. I like black tea, _____ my husband doesn't. He likes green tea.

    (a) either　(b) so　(c) but

11. She doesn't like cheese, and _____ does her sister.

    (a) either　(b) neither　(c) so

12. A: I can't swim.

    B: Me _____.

    (a) either　(b) too　(c) neither

13. A: I must go home now.

    B: Me _____.

    (a) too　(b) either　(c) neither

14. I can't speak French, _____ can I speak German.

    (a) so　(b) but　(c) nor

15. Last night I didn't do my homework, _____ did I play the piano.

    (a) and　(b) nor　(c) yet

16. We were neither happy _____ sad.

    (a) or　(b) nor　(c) but

17. I don't like horror movies(恐怖片), and neither _____ he.

    (a) is　(b) do　(c) does

18. I went to KTV last night, and so _____ she.

    (a) does　(b) did　(c) was

19. Peter has an Iranian friend(伊朗的朋友), and so _____ I.

    (a) do　(b) has　(c) am

20. I've never been to Brazil, neither _____ he.

    (a) does　(b) is　(c) has

10-5-2 填填看（＊注意：句子第一個字母要用大寫。）

> as long as,　in order to,　because of,　either,　wherever,　after,
> whenever,　even though,　while,　unless,　whereas,　once, if

1. ＿＿＿＿＿＿ he is not very interested in economics, he chose it as his major.

2. I will buy an MP3 ＿＿＿＿＿ the price goes down to NT$500.

3. ＿＿＿＿＿ the bad weather, we cancelled our trip to Taitung.

4. ＿＿＿＿＿ you finish this book, let me know. I will buy you another one.

5. I've found an apartment, ＿＿＿＿＿ they are still searching.

6. The dog finds the keys ＿＿＿＿＿ its master hides them.

7. ＿＿＿＿＿ reading his biography, she understood the writer better.

8. ＿＿＿＿＿ I find the right person to adopt my cat, I will keep it.

9. ＿＿＿＿＿ find the right owner for my cat, I surf the Internet almost every day.

10. ＿＿＿＿＿ I find a job, I will move away from home.

11. They like hip-hop music, ＿＿＿＿＿ we like classical music.

12. I don't read ＿＿＿＿＿ science fiction（科幻小說）or fantasy（奇幻小說）.

10-5-3 問答

1. What did the writer dream of last night?

　＿＿＿＿＿＿＿＿＿＿＿＿＿＿＿＿＿＿＿＿＿＿＿＿＿＿＿＿＿＿＿

2. In his dream, what was with Inky?

　＿＿＿＿＿＿＿＿＿＿＿＿＿＿＿＿＿＿＿＿＿＿＿＿＿＿＿＿＿＿＿

3. What woke the writer up?

　＿＿＿＿＿＿＿＿＿＿＿＿＿＿＿＿＿＿＿＿＿＿＿＿＿＿＿＿＿＿＿

4. What did the writer see when he woke up?

　＿＿＿＿＿＿＿＿＿＿＿＿＿＿＿＿＿＿＿＿＿＿＿＿＿＿＿＿＿＿＿

5. What was his dad's reaction（反應）when he saw the two cats?

　＿＿＿＿＿＿＿＿＿＿＿＿＿＿＿＿＿＿＿＿＿＿＿＿＿＿＿＿＿＿＿

6.　What was his mom's reaction when she saw the two cats?

_____

7.　Why did the writer quickly jump out of his bed?

_____

8.　What did the writer do with the kitten's pictures?

_____

9.　Where did the writer receive messages from?

_____

10.　Who was the adopter the writer chose?

_____

11.　How did the writer decide who could adopt his kitten?

_____

10-5-4 改錯

1.　Although I want to keep the kitten, but my parents won't allow me to do so.
2.　Inky came back, and so does the kitten.
3.　I don't want to adopt a cat, and either does he.
4.　Because my parents didn't want to keep the kitten, so I tried to find a person to adopt her.
5.　A: I don't like cats. B: Me too.
6.　I would like a cup of tea, and so does my husband.
7.　I was sick, I went to school.
8.　Even though it is very cold, I not wearing a coat.
9.　Because of he was tired, he went to bed early.
10.　We live in an apartment, and so is he.
11.　I can't ride a motorcycle, nor can't I drive a car.
12.　He can't play the piano, and his brother can't, too.

10-5-5英文該怎麼寫？

1. Hello Kitty 是有名的日本漫畫人物。

　　_____

2. 她不只喜歡打籃球，還喜歡打羽毛球（badminton）。

　　_____

3. 我收到來自伊朗、巴西和南非來的訊息。

　　_____

4. 爸爸堅定地跟我說：「我們不能收留任何貓！」

　　_____

5. 她正在考慮要不要去車站去見他。

　　_____

6. 我喜歡看科幻片，我的男朋友也喜歡。

　　_____

7. 我不會騎腳踏車，我妹妹也不會。

　　_____

8. 我決定走路上學，我的朋友們也決定如此。

　　_____

9. 只要他願意收養我的貓，我會立刻帶去給他。

　　_____

10. 我把所有我的貓的照片都波在網站上（on the website）。

　　_____

第十一課 Unit 11

冠詞

互動光碟

英文裡的冠詞雖然小，又只有兩類：不定冠詞(a, an)和定冠詞(the)，不過卻讓台灣學生頭痛不已；因為中文和俄文、日文一樣，沒有冠詞這種詞性，學生初學英文時自然感覺陌生，有時即使學了一陣子英文，還是弄不清楚什麼名詞前面不必加冠詞，什麼名詞前該加冠詞？如果需要用冠詞，什麼時候該用定冠詞，什麼時候用不定冠詞？如果用不定冠詞，什麼時候用 a，什麼時候用 an？

現在讓我們來一一回答上面的問題：

I. 什麼名詞前面通常不加冠詞？

1. 不可數名詞前面通常不加冠詞，例如：

🔊 She listens to music every night.
她每晚聽音樂。

🔊 I drink green tea every morning.
我每天早上喝綠茶。

🔊 They search for information on the Internet.
他們在網路上搜尋資訊。

　＊ 注意：關係代名詞特別指出來的不可數名詞可以加定冠詞 the，
　　如：

🔊 I like the tea(which) he made.
我喜歡喝他泡的茶。

2. 複數名詞前通常不加冠詞，例如：

🔊 I like dogs.(泛指所有的狗。)
我喜歡狗。

🔊 Clothes are expensive in Paris.
巴黎的衣服很貴。

🔊 Books are everywhere in her room.

她的房間到處都是書。

　＊注意：關係代名詞特別指出來的複數名詞可以加定冠詞 the，
　　　如：

🔊 The dogs (which) she found on the street are very ill.

她在街上發現的狗病得很重。

3. 人名、頭銜前通常不加冠詞。例如：

🔊 Professor Lee will give a speech today.

李教授今天要演講。

🔊 Doctor Wong is very patient.

王醫生非常有耐心。

🔊 Today is Aunt Lucy's birthday.

今天是露西阿姨的生日。

4. 星期、月份、節日前不加冠詞，例如：

🔊 I have six classes on Thursday.

我星期四有六節課。

🔊 Our summer vacation is from July to September.

我們的暑假從七月放到九月。

🔊 We don't have class on New Year's Day.

我們元旦不上課。

5. 三餐 (breakfast, lunch, dinner) 前不用加冠詞。

🔊 What do you have for breakfast?

你早餐吃什麼？

　＊注意：關係代名詞特別指出來的三餐可以加定冠詞 the，如：

The breakfast (which) you made for me was delicious.

你幫我做的早餐很好吃。

6. 各種球類前不必加冠詞，例如：

go bowling 打保齡球

play basketball 打籃球

play ping pong (play table tennis) 打乒乓球

play baseball 打棒球

play softball 打壘球

play tennis 打網球

play volleyball 打排球

play soccer 踢足球

play badminton 打羽毛球

play pool 打撞球

7. 習慣用語中的名詞前不加冠詞，例如：

at home 在家

at work 在工作

in class 上課

go to bed 去睡覺

go to school 上學

go to church 上教堂

be in bed 在睡覺

by bike 騎單車（by taxi, by bus, by train, on foot）

on TV 在電視上

on duty 值班

on leave 請假中

in love 戀愛中

in debt 負債

in trouble 有麻煩

in hospital 住院

8. 地名、學校名、公園名、車站名、機場名、國家名、語言、星座和行星前不加冠詞，例如：

Sun Moon Lake 日月潭

Mount Ali 阿里山

Taichung Railway Station 台中火車站

Central Park 中央公園

Kennedy Airport 甘迺迪機場

Sixth Avenue 第六街

Harvard University 哈佛大學

Arabic 阿拉伯語，Thai 泰語，Russian 俄語，Italian 義大利語，Cambodian 柬埔寨語，French 法語，German 德語，Spanish 西班牙語

Mars 火星，Venus 金星，Saturn 土星，Jupiter 木星，Mercury 水星

Taurus 金牛座，Gemini 雙魚座，Cancer 巨蟹座

*注意：Russian 俄語不加 the，但是 the Russian language 要加 the；America 不加 the，但是 the United States of America(the USA)要加 the。

II. 什麼時候用定冠詞 the？

1. 之前描述過的名詞，再出現、與不定冠詞作對比時用定冠
   詞，例如：

- I have a dog and a cat. The dog is black, but the cat is white.
  我有一隻狗和一隻貓。狗是黑的，而貓是白的。

- A girl and a boy are sitting on the bench. The girl looks angry, and
  the boy looks upset.
  一個女孩和男孩坐在長凳上。女孩看起來很生氣，男孩看
  起來很沮喪。

2. 指特定事物時，用定冠詞，例如：

- She bought some books for the children in the kindergarten.
  她買了些書給幼稚園的小朋友。
  (特指幼稚園的小孩，用定冠詞。)

- Children usually learn faster than adults.
  孩子通常比大人學得快。
  (泛指所有的小孩，不用定冠詞。)

- Please pass the sugar to me.
  請把那個糖遞給我。(指特定的糖，用定冠詞。)

- Sugar is bad for you.
  糖對你不好。(泛指所有的糖，不用定冠詞。)

3. 談話的雙方在同一地點所指的人或事物，用定冠詞，例如：

- Before you leave the classroom, please turn the light off.
  你離開教室前，請關燈。

♪ <u>The floor</u> in the kitchen is very dirty.
廚房的地板很髒。

♪ <u>The teacher</u> asks students to look at the blackboard.
老師要學生看黑板。

4. 樂器前加定冠詞，例如：

🔈 play the violin 拉小提琴

play the piano 彈鋼琴

play the organ 彈風琴

play the flute 吹笛子

play the guitar 彈吉他

play the harmonica 吹口琴

play the saxophone 吹薩克斯風

5. 表示時間或地點的某些習慣用法，加定冠詞，例如：

🔈 in the morning / in the afternoon / in the evening 早上／中午
／晚上

at the moment 目前

for the time being 暫時

in the past 過去

the day before 前天

the following day 次日

on the same day 同一天

at the same time 同時

on the left / right 在左／右邊

at the corner 在轉角處

6. 氣候或自然環境的名詞前，用定冠詞，例如：

🔊 the rain 雨，the wind 風，the sea 海

in the rain 在雨中，in the sun 在太陽下，in the shade 在陰
涼處，in the dark 在黑暗中，in the moonlight 在月光下

the earth 地球，the sun 太陽，the moon 月亮，the sky 天
空，the world 世界，the universe 宇宙

7. 國籍前面要加定冠詞，例如：

🔊 the Chinese 中國人

the Arabs 阿拉伯人

the Americans 美國人

the Romans 羅馬人

the Greeks 希臘人

the Filipinos 菲律賓人

the Thais 泰國人

8. the＋形容詞＝某一類的人，例如：

🔊 the poor 窮人

the rich 富人

the unemployed 失業的人

the blind 盲人

the deaf 聾人

the old 老人

the young 年輕人

9. 江河、海洋、群島、沙漠、山脈、湖泊等專有名詞前，加定冠詞，例如：

> the Yellow River 黃河
>
> the Pacific Ocean 太平洋
>
> the Taiwan Strait 台灣海峽
>
> the Sahara 撒哈拉沙漠
>
> the Himalayas 喜馬拉雅山脈

10. 表示某姓氏的全家人，加定冠詞(注意，家人是多數，要加s)，例如：

> the Lins 林家人

11. 表示某個時代或某個歷史事件，加定冠詞，例如：

> the Renaissance 文藝復興時期
>
> the 228 Incident 228事件
>
> the Cultural Revolution 文化大革命

12. 名詞＋of＋名詞的前面，要加定冠詞，例如

> the president of Russia 俄國總統
>
> the Minister of Education 教育部長
>
> the University of Cambridge 劍橋大學
>
> the Bank of Taiwan 台灣銀行

13. 報紙或雜誌名稱前，加定冠詞，例如：

> the Bible 聖經
>
> the *United Daily News* 《聯合報》
>
> the *Taipei Times* 《台北時報》

the *New York Times* 《紐約時報》

the *Economist* 《經濟學人週刊》

14. 政府機構、組織團體、政黨名稱前，加定冠詞，例如：

🔈 the Ministry of Education 教育部

the Central Weather Bureau 中央氣象局

the Red Cross Society 紅十字會

the Conservative Party 保守黨

15. 體育館、博物館、美術館、劇院前，加定冠詞，例如：

🔈 the British Museum 大英博物館

the National Palace Museum 故宮博物館

the Taipei Art Museum 台北市立美術館

III. 什麼時候用不定冠詞？

1. 第一次提到單數可數名詞時，前面要加不定冠詞，例如：

🔈 I bought <u>an apartment</u> on Renai Road. Later I rented <u>the apartment</u> to three college students.
我在仁愛路買了一棟公寓。後來我把這棟公寓租給三個大學生。

2. 指某一類的人或事物，前面要加不定冠詞(a 指 any 任何一個)，例如：

🔈 <u>A civil servant</u> is a person who works for the government.
公務員是為政府做事的人。

🔈 <u>A remedy</u> is something used to cure illness or pain.
療法是用來治癒疾病或疼痛的方法。

3. 指某人、某物或某件事情時，前面要加不定冠詞，例如：

🦻 I met an old friend on the bus.
我在公車上遇到一位老朋友。

🦻 She bought a new dress.
她買了一件新洋裝。

4. 與數量詞、單位、價格、速度連用時，前面要加不定冠詞，例如：

🦻 I drink a cup of coffee every day.
我每天喝一杯咖啡。

🦻 He bought a dozen toothbrushes.
他買了一打牙刷。

🦻 It takes me half an hour to get to school.
我上學要花半個小時。

🦻 This kind of tea costs me a hundred dollars a kilo.
這種茶一公斤要花我一百美元。

5. 與某些疾病連用時，前面要加不定冠詞，例如：

🦻 have a cold 感冒

have a sore throat 喉嚨發炎

have a headache 頭痛

have a toothache 牙痛

have a stomachache 胃痛

have a backache 背痛

have a fever 發燒

6. 慣用語前面要加不定冠詞，例如：

🎵 It's a pity that you can't go with us.
可惜你不能跟我們去。

🎵 I will call you in a day or two.
我一兩天內會打電話給你。

🎵 Once upon a time there was a prince.
很久很久以前有一個王子。

🎵 Let's take a walk after dinner.
我們晚餐後去散步吧。

🎵 I am on a diet.
我在節食。

7. 與專有名詞連用前面要加不定冠詞，例如：

🎵 She is a Buddhist.
她是佛教徒。

🎵 She is an Indonesian.
她是印尼人。

🎵 A Mr. Wong is here waiting for you.
有位王先生在這等你。

IV. 什麼時候用 a？什麼時候用 an？

1. 字的第一個字母是子音（除了 a, e, i, o, u 五個母音之外都是子音），前面要用 a，例如：

a cat, a dog, a book, a rabbit 中 c, d, b, r 都是子音。

2. 字的第一個字母看起來是母音，但發音卻是子音，前面要用 a，例如：

a university, a uniform, a European 中 u, u, e 看似都是母音字，但發音卻是子音[j]

3. 字的第一個字母是母音(a, e, i, o, u)，前面要用 an，例如：

an orange, an apple, an elephant, an umbrella

4. 字的第一個字母看起來是子音，但子音不發音，而由母音開頭，前面要用 an，例如：

an hour, an honor program, an honest man(這些字的 h 都不發音。)

朗讀 CD 第 7 軌

互動光碟

11-1 生字 Vocabulary

net friend	(n.)網友
alley	(n.)巷子
draw a lot	(ph.)抽籤
relief	(n.)寬心；(v.) relieve(relieve, relieved, relieved)
hang around	(ph.)逛一逛，晃一晃
stroll	(v.)閒逛(stroll, strolled, strolled)
a group of	(ph.)一群
shopkeeper	(n.)店主
customer	(n.)顧客
mountain bike	(n.)登山腳踏車
foldable bike	(n.)摺疊腳踏車
bicycle-built-for-two	(n.)協力車
spot	(v.)注意到(spot, spotted, spotted)
lady's bike	(n.)淑女車
bargain	(v.)討價還價(bargain, bargained, bargained)

n.＝名詞　ph.＝詞組　v.＝動詞　adv.＝副詞　adj.＝形容詞

obviously	(adv.)顯然地
cut	(v.)減少(cut, cut, cut)
give in	(ph.)讓步(give, gave, given)
discount	(n.)折扣
scooter	(n.)機車
second-hand	(adj.)二手的
sigh	(v.)嘆氣(sigh, sighed, sighed)
gas prices	(n.)油價
hit an all-time high	(ph.)飆到最高

朗讀 CD 第 8 軌

互動光碟

11-2 課文 Text

I met both of my **net friends** at a coffee shop[1] on the corner of a small **alley**. As soon as we stepped into the coffee shop, both of them claimed[2] that they were animal lovers and wanted to have my cat. This was one of the hardest[3] decisions I've ever had to make in my life. In the end, I asked them to **draw lots**. The single mom got my cat.

I felt a big **relief**[4], so I decided to **hang around** for a while before going home for lunch. **Strolling**[5] along the busiest street in downtown Tainan, I saw **a group of** people in front of a bike shop. The **shopkeeper** was busily introducing **customers** to **mountain bikes**, **foldable bikes**, and **bicycles-built-for-two**. Among the customers, I surprisingly **spotted**[6] my parents.

Mom was excitedly[7] showing me a beautiful purple **lady's bike**. Dad, however, was **bargaining** with the shopkeeper. **Obviously**, he wanted him to **cut** the price. The shopkeeper finally **gave in**[8]. He decided to give Dad a 20% **discount**[9] since Dad bought two bikes at the same time. When they walked their new bikes out and were ready to ride them home, Dad suggested[10] I sell my **scooter** and buy a **second-hand**[11] bike instead. He **sighed**, "**Gas prices** just **hit an all-time high**[12]. Sooner or later, no one will be able to afford to drive a car!"

11-3 課文翻譯

　　我在小巷轉角的一家咖啡館見到我的兩位網友。我們一踏進咖啡館，他們兩個都立即聲稱自己愛動物也想要我的貓。這是我這輩子中最難做的決定之一。最後我要他們抽籤，結果單親媽媽得到我的貓。

　　我大大鬆了一口氣，於是決定先在外面晃一晃再回家吃中飯，沿著台南市區最熱鬧的街道閒逛時，我看到一群人在腳踏車店前。店老闆正忙著介紹顧客登山腳踏車、小摺，還有協力車。在那群顧客中，我居然看到了我的爸媽！

　　媽媽興奮地秀一台漂亮的紫色淑女車給我看，而爸爸卻在跟老闆討價還價。顯然他要老闆降價。老闆最後讓步，決定給爸爸打八折，因為爸爸一次買了兩台車。他們推著腳踏車出來，準備騎車回家時，爸建議我賣掉機車改買二手腳踏車。他嘆口氣說：「油價剛飆到前所未有的高點。遲早沒人開得起車了！」

11-4 解析 Language Focus

互動光碟

1. 第一次提到 coffee shop 時，用冠詞 a，當 coffee shop 再度出現時，用冠詞 the

   section 段，lane 巷，alley 弄

   如果中文地址是台北市忠孝東路三段 251 巷 5 弄8-2號，因為英文寫法與中文地址次序相反，所以英文會寫成：

   8-2, Alley 5, Lane 251, Section 3

   Zhongxiao East Road

   Taipei

2. 這句是從直接敘述句 They claimed, "We are animal lovers." 改為間接敘述句 They claimed that they were animal lovers.（16 課有更詳細的說明）

   以下是從直接問句／句子改為間接句子的例子：

   He said, "I went to a great restaurant."

   　　他說：「我去了一間很棒的餐廳。」

   He said that he had been to a great restaurant.

   　　他說他去了一家很棒的餐廳。

   He asked me, "Are you going to see a movie now?"

   　　他問我：「你現在是不是要去看電影了？」

   He asked me if I am going to see a movie now.

   　　他問我現在是不是要去看電影了？

🦻 He told me, "Don't eat the French fries on the table."

他告訴我：「不要吃桌上的薯條。」

He told me not to eat the French fries on the table.

他告訴我不要吃桌上的薯條。

（French fries 原本不加 the，但特別指出桌上的薯條，要加 the）

3. the hardest＝the most difficult

   one of... 其中之一，後面的名詞 decisions 要用複數。

4. relief 寬心（名詞），relieve 使放心；減輕（動詞）

   🦻 His winning a scholarship is a great relief to his family.
   他拿到了獎學金，家人大感輕鬆。

   🦻 Hearing he had won a scholarship, his family felt relieved.
   聽到他得到了獎學金，他的家人鬆了一口氣。

   🦻 Drugs can help relieve my pain.
   藥物幫我減輕痛楚。

5. 這是將兩句主詞相同的句子，併為一句的例子。

   🦻 I strolled along the busiest street in downtown Tainan.
   　 I saw a group of people in front of a bike shop.

   →Strolling along the busiest street in downtown Tainan, I saw a group of people
   　in front of a bike shop.

6. spot＝notice 注意到（動詞），spot 地點（名詞）

   🦻 The teacher failed to spot this grammatical error.
   老師沒注意到這個文法錯誤。

   🦻 Sun Moon Lake is one of the most famous scenic spots in Taiwan.
   日月潭是台灣最有名的景點之一。

7. excitedly 興奮地（副詞），excited 感到興奮的（形容詞），excite 使興奮（動詞），excitement 興奮（名詞）

   🦻 She is excitedly telling me the good news.
   她興奮地告訴我這個好消息。

◊ Hearing this good news, she <u>felt excited</u>.
聽到這個好消息，她覺得很興奮。

◊ All my students are in a state of great <u>excitement</u>.
我所有的學生都處在興奮狀態。

8.   give in 讓步，give up 放棄

◊ The employer finally <u>gave in</u> and agreed to employee pay raises.
雇主終於讓步，同意員工加薪。

◊ He will never <u>give up</u> learning English.
他絕不放棄學習英文。

9.   discount 打折，20% off 打八折，50% off 打對折

◊ Can I get a discount if I buy three cans of peaches?
我如果買三罐桃子有沒有折扣？

◊ If you buy a whole case of kiwis, you will get 50% off.
如果你買整箱奇異果，可以打對折。

10.   suggest 這個動詞的特殊用法我們在高級本上冊曾詳加說明，現在再提醒讀者，suggest 後面不能接受詞，如：I suggested her (x).

◊ I suggested she (should) start to ride a bike.
我建議她開始騎單車。

◊ He suggested I find a job first.
他建議我先找個工作。

◊ They suggested we go to graduate school.
他們建議我們讀研究所。

11.   second-hand car＝used car(中古車)，brand new car(全新的車)

12.   at an all-time high 最高點，at an all-time low 最低點

◊ The president's popularity is at an all-time low.
總統的聲望降到最低點。

11-5-1 選選看

1. This is _____ easy question, but most students failed to answer it.
    (a) a　(b) an　(c) X

2. Amy is _____ smartest student in our class.
    (a) a　(b) an　(c) the

3. Is there _____ restroom（廁所）near here?
    (a) a　(b) an　(c) the

4. _____ apple a day keeps _____ doctor away.
    (a) A, a　(b) An, the　(c) An, an

5. This summer vacation we spent a lot of time swimming in _____ sea.
    (a) a　(b) X　(c) the

6. My students never listen to _____ classical music（古典音樂）.
    (a) a　(b) X　(c) the

7. It was _____ excellent movie.
    (a) a　(b) an　(c) the

8. I usually have _____ dinner at 6:30 P.M.
    (a) a　(b) X　(c) the

9. _____ dinner party my co-worker held last night was wonderful.
    (a) A　(b) X　(c) The

10. I bought _____ umbrella at the night market three days ago.
    (a) a　(b) an　(c) X

11. Would you mind turning off _____ lights in the living room when you leave?

　　(a) a　(b) X　(c) the

12. Come in! _____ water is very warm.

　　(a) A　(b) X　(c) The

13. I've been looking for _____ job for quite a while.

　　(a) A　(b) X　(c) The

14. I had to take _____ taxi in order to catch the 7:45 high speed train.

　　(a) a　(b) X　(c) the

15. I need to take _____ break(休息一下) before continuing my work.

　　(a) a　(b) X　(c) the

16. I would like _____ glass of orange juice, please.

　　(a) A　(b) an　(c) The

17. May I have _____ glass of apple juice on the counter(流理台)?

　　(a) a　(b) X　(c) the

18. I first went there by _____ bus, then I took _____ train.

　　(a) X, X　(b) X, the　(c) a, a

19. Do you often go to _____ church?

　　(a) a　(b) X　(c) the

20. The museum is on the first road on _____ right.

　　(a) a　(b) X　(c) the

21. I have to go to _____ bank to withdraw some money(提錢).

　　(a) an　(b) X　(c) the

22. Henry is in _____ class right now. He can't answer your call.

　　(a) a　(b) X　(c) the

23. I like _____ Indian food, but I don't like Bollywood movies(印度寶萊塢歌舞片).

　　(a) a　(b) X　(c) the

24. I had _____ terrible headache last night.
    (a) a (b) X (c) the

25. He's _____ very firm Catholic(虔誠的天主教徒).
    (a) a (b) X (c) the

26. Have you been to _____ National Palace Museum?
    (a) a (b) X (c) the

27. _____ Smiths will visit us tonight.
    (a) A (b) X (c) The

28. They live in _____ eastern part of Taiwan.
    (a) a (b) X (c) the

29. These apples are from _____ South America.
    (a) a (b) X (c) the

30. Paris is _____ capital(首都) of France.
    (a) a (b) X (c) the

11-5-2 填填看(＊注意：句子第一個字母要用大寫。)

```
a   an   the   X
```

1. This handbag was designed by _____ famous Taiwanese fashion designer.

2. I will buy _____ iPod when the price goes down to NT$1000.

3. Do you have _____ eraser(橡皮擦) that I can borrow?

4. _____ pandas(熊貓) are endangered animals(瀕臨絕種的動物).

5. _____ ant is _____ insect(昆蟲).

6. He is _____ honest person.

7. John wants to be _____ engineer after graduating from college.

8. Mother Teresa(德蕾莎修女) helped for _____ poor.

9. I'm on _____ diet. Please no _____ sugar for me.

10. I am staying at _____ hotel near _____ Tamshui River(淡水河).

11. _____ friend of mine will join us tonight.

12. I can't remember ＿＿＿ exact date of ＿＿＿ her birthday.

13. I don't like ＿＿＿ soccer(足球).

14. She knows how to play ＿＿＿ piano.

15. ＿＿＿ water is dirty. Don't drink it.

16. ＿＿＿ price of gas keeps rising.

17. ＿＿＿ amazing thing happened to her last night.

18. She doesn't eat ＿＿＿ red meat.

19. She hung ＿＿＿ old dress on ＿＿＿ balcony.

20. May I borrow ＿＿＿ English dictionary from you?

11-5-3問答

1. What did his net friends say when they met him in the coffee shop?

   _____

2. What did the writer do to decide who would get the cat?

   _____

3. Who got the cat in the end?

   _____

4. How did the writer feel after solving the problem of the cat(解決了貓的問題)?

   _____

5. What did the writer see while strolling along the streets?

   _____

6. What kinds of bikes did the shopkeeper show to the customers?

   _____

7. Among the customers, who did the writer spot?

   _____

8. What kind of bike did his mom buy?

   _____

9. Why did his dad bargain with the shop owner?

_____

10. How much of a discount did his dad get?

_____

11. Why did his dad suggest he should get rid of his scooter?

_____

12. What kind of vehicle（車）did his dad suggest he buy?

_____

11-5-4 改錯

1. Is there post office near here? I need to go to the post office.
2. My professor is an European.
3. Furnitures is getting more and more expensive.
4. Please give me an advice.
5. I love the 70s（70年代）music.
6. He lives in a old house.
7. He is a my friend.
8. I need an information about that singer's birthday.
9. I am tired. I need to go to the bed now.
10. It has been a extremely hot summer vacation.
11. What did you do with ice cream I bought?
12. I would like you to meet the Dr. Wong.
13. I was surprised to find out that he can speak Thai language.
14. I took a trip to USA last summer.
15. In a day or two, I will tell you a good news.

11-5-5英文該怎麼寫？

1. 這是我一生中最快樂的一天。

   _____

2. 我們昨晚去打保齡球。

   _____

3. 上星期我和男友騎協力車遊墾丁（toured Kenting）。

   _____

4. 考完高中入學考（the High School Entrance Exam），我感覺鬆了一口氣。

   _____

5. 我用九五折買到這輛摺疊腳踏車。

   _____

6. 他興奮地秀給我看他全新的（brand new）摩托車。

   _____

7. 生活費（the cost of living）飆到最高點。

   _____

8. 在所有學生當中，我一眼就注意到（spotted）那個菲律賓人。

   _____

9. 所有失業的人都找到了工作。

   _____

10. 他建議我先找份工作。

   _____

第十二課 Unit 12

子句

互動光碟

　　一個句子中的小句子，叫做「子句」，又叫「句中句」。例如：

> I don't know what her name is.
> 我不知道她的名字是什麼。(I don't know 是主要的句子，what her name is 是附屬它的子句。)

> I wonder where I can find her.
> 我在想哪裡可以找到她。(I wonder 是主要的句子，where I can find her 是附屬它的子句。)

> This is the newspaper that she is looking for.
> 這就是她正在找的報紙。(This is the newspaper 是主要的句子，that she is looking for 是附屬它的子句。)

　　子句可依其在句子中擔任的角色，分為名詞子句、副詞子句及形容詞子句：

I. 名詞子句：子句當成主詞、受詞及補充主詞(又叫做補語)的句子來使用，例如：

當成主詞

> What I bought for her was a book.
> 我買給她的是一本書。(名詞子句 What I bought for her 當主詞用。)

當成受詞

> I don't know which book he has read.
> 我不知道他讀了哪本書。(名詞子句 which book he has read 當動詞 know 的受詞用。)

當成補語

🎧 The problem is <u>who should pay the bill</u>.

問題是誰該付帳。（名詞子句 who should pay the bill 補充說明主詞 problem。）

II. 副詞子句：句子的功能如同副詞，用來形容主要子句全句、動詞、形容詞和副詞。

形容動詞

🎧 I'll <u>stay</u> home <u>whether it rains or not</u>.

無論是否下雨，我都會待在家裡。（副詞子句 whether it rains or not 形容主要子句 I'll stay home。）

形容形容詞

🎧 I am very <u>tired</u> <u>because last night I stayed up late</u>.

我很累，因為昨天太晚睡。（副詞子句 because last night I stayed up late 形容形容詞 tired。）

形容副詞

🎧 She speaks so <u>fast</u> <u>that I can't understand her</u>.

她說得太快，快到我都聽不懂。（副詞子句 that I can't understand her 形容副詞 fast。）

III. 形容詞子句：句子的功能如同形容詞，用來形容名詞。形容詞子句又叫做關係子句。我們常用一個形容詞形容人或物，如 a nice person 一個好人，a red dress 一件紅色的洋裝，但有時候我們也會用一長串的詞來形容一個人或物，如「住在我家隔壁的女士」、「跑得很快的狗」，這時候就需要用關係子句來形容「女士」、「狗」這些名詞，如：

🖉 The woman <u>who lives next door to us</u> is very nice.
住在我們家隔壁的女士非常好。（who lives next door to us 形容 the woman。）

🖉 The dog <u>which runs very fast</u> is mine.
這隻跑得很快的狗是我養的。（which runs very fast 形容 the dog。）

* 注意：以上關係子句中的 who 和 which 叫做關係代名詞，它必須緊跟著前面的名詞，亦稱為先行詞（the woman, the dog），它的作用在取代、描述或形容前面的先行詞，如果先行詞是單數，關係代名詞後面的動詞須為單數形，如：lives, runs。

以上兩個例句其實都是由兩個句子合成一句的：

👂 The woman is very nice.
The woman lives next door to us.

→ The woman who lives next door to us is very nice.

👂 The dog is mine.
The dog runs very fast.

→ The dog which runs very fast is mine.

關係子句通常是以關係代名詞，如：who、 that、which、whose、whom 開頭的形容詞子句，用來描述說話者所說的人或事物。我們現在分別以例句說明它們各自的用法：

1. who 用來取代「人」，在子句中當主詞用。例如：

🖉 The boy <u>who</u> fell from the bike is my son.
從腳踏車上摔下來的是我的兒子。（who＝the boy）

🖉 Ms. Huang, <u>who</u> interviewed our president, is an anchorwoman.
採訪我們校長的黃女士是新聞主播。（who＝Ms. Huang）

A customer is someone <u>who</u> buys something at a store.
顧客就是在店裡買東西的人。（who＝someone）

2. which 用來取代「事、物」或「動物」，在子句中可以當主詞、受詞、也可以當代名詞(代表這件事)，例如：

當主詞：

Who owns that house <u>which</u> has a red roof?
誰擁有那棟紅屋頂的房子？（which 當主詞＝that house）

當受詞：

There is a book <u>which</u> your aunt might be interested in.
有本書你的姑姑也許會有興趣。（which 當受詞＝a book）

＊注意：be interested in 是固定用法，不能拆開。

（×）Here is a book in which your aunt might be interested.

當代名詞：

He passed the entrance exam, <u>which</u> surprised everyone.
他居然通過了入學考試，讓每個人跌破了眼鏡。（which 當代名詞 it，指的是 He passed the entrance exam. 這件事。）

3. whom 當受詞用，通常可以用 who 取代。

The man <u>whom</u>(who) you met yesterday is my brother.
你昨天見到的那個人是我的哥哥。（whom＝the man，是 met 的受詞。）

The man <u>whom</u>(who) I fell in love with is younger than I am.
我愛上的男人年紀比我小。（whom＝the man，是 fall in love with 的受詞）

*who 在某種情況下不能取代 whom，請比較下面兩個例句：

〽 I don't know the girl whom（who）he danced with.

＝ I don't know the girl with whom he danced.

　我不認識跟他跳舞的女孩。（*注意：第二句介系詞 with 後面的受詞，只能用 whom，不能用 who 取代。）

4. that（可以取代 which 和 who / whom）

〽 Have you found the umbrella that you lost?

　你找到你弄丟的雨傘了嗎？（that＝which＝the umbrella）

〽 The dentist that you go to happens to be a friend of mine.

　你去看的那個牙醫正好是我一個朋友。（that＝who / whom＝the dentist）

〽 She works for the bakery that makes whole wheat bread.

　她在那家做全麥麵包的麵包店做事。（that＝which＝bakery）

* 注意：that 在下列情況下不能取代 which / who / whom

a. 介系詞後面的 which 或 whom 不能用 that 取代，如：

〽 This is the house in which he lives.

　這是他住的房子。（in which 不能改為 in that。）

〽 She is the girl with whom he danced.

　她就是跟他跳舞的女孩。（with whom 不能改為 with that。）

b. 逗點後面的 which 或 who 不能用 that 取代，如：

〽 Mr. Lin, who is the owner of the pet shop, showed us an adorable kitten.

　寵物店老闆林先生給我們看一隻可愛的小貓。（who 不能改為 that。）

◈ My teacher lent me *The Lord of the Rings*, <u>which</u> is difficult to read.
我的老師借給我的《魔戒》不容易讀。(which 不能改為 that。)

c. those 後面的 who 不能改為 that，如：

◈ Those <u>who</u> eat breakfast every day tend to be more energetic.
每天吃早餐的人往往比較精力充沛。(who 不能改為 that。)

◈ Those <u>who</u> like reading novels have a large vocabulary.
喜歡讀小說的人知道的生字比較多。(who 不能改為 that。)

＊注意：在下列情況下只能用 that，不能用 which / who / whom：

a. 先行詞前有最高級形容詞，只能用 that，例如：

◈ She is the smartest person <u>that</u> I have ever met.
她是我遇過最聰明的人。

b. 先行詞前有序數(the first, the second, the last...)，例如：

◈ She is the first girl <u>that</u> won the chess championship.
她是第一個拿到西洋棋比賽冠軍的女孩。

c. 先行詞前有 the only, the same, any, every, all...，例如：

◈ All the girls <u>that</u> play soccer can join the game.
所有踢足球的女孩們都可以參加比賽。

d. 主要句子是以 who 或 which 開頭的疑問句，例如：

◈ Who are the girls <u>that</u> play soccer?
踢足球的女孩們是誰？

◈ Which is the book <u>that</u> you chose yesterday?
你昨天選的是哪一本書？

5. whose 代替 his / her / their / its，用來當作所有格代名詞。如：

　　◎ I adopted a cat <u>whose</u> tail is very short.
　　　　我認養了一隻尾巴很短的貓。（whose＝its）

　　◎ Do you know the girl <u>whose</u> brother won a bronze medal in the
　　　　Olympics?（a gold medal 金牌、a silver medal 銀牌）
　　　　你認識那個哥哥得了奧運銅牌的女孩嗎？。（whose＝her）

　＊注意：whose 通常指人和動物的所有格，東西的所有格通常不
　　用 whose，如：

　　（×）I saw a house <u>whose</u> roof is purple.

　　這句英文可以改寫成：

　　◎ I saw a house which has a purple roof.

＊注意：who's＝who is，跟 whose 的意思不同。

　　除了一般常用的關係代名詞 who, whom, which, whose, that 之
外，以下關係代名詞 where, when, why, what 也會在關係子句中出
現：

6. where 等於介系詞＋which，表示地方、場所，例如：

　　◎ The shop <u>where</u> I usually buy organic food is near here.
　　　　我常買有機食物的店就在這附近。（where＝at which）

　　◎ I revisited the town <u>where</u> I was born.
　　　　我重訪我出生的小鎮。（where＝in which）

7. when 等於介系詞＋which，表示時間，例如：

　　◎ I'll never forget the day when I first met you.
　　　　我絕對忘不了第一次見到你的那一天。（when＝on which）

🔊 Chinese New Year is a holiday <u>when</u> families like to gather together.

農曆新年是家人喜歡團聚在一起的節日。(when＝which)

8. why 等於 for which，表示原因，例如：

🔊 The reason <u>why</u> he couldn't come was a mystery.

他不能來的原因是個謎。(why＝for which)

9. what 等於 the thing(s)＋which，本身已有先行詞，故前面不會有先行詞，例如：

🔊 Please tell me <u>what</u> is on your mind.

請告訴我你心裡在想什麼。

🔊 I don't like <u>what</u> she has told me.

我不喜歡她告訴我的事情。

關係子句又可以分為限定子句和非限定子句。

a. 限定子句：如果 which／who 前面的名詞「沒有明確指出」是什麼東西或是誰，須用限定子句。限定子句的前面「沒有逗點」，如：

🔊 The woman <u>who</u> lives next door is a teacher.

這個住在隔壁的女人是老師。

這個女人(the woman)是誰我們不知道，所以須說清楚是我家隔壁的那位女人。who lives next door 這個子句很重要，如果不寫，我們就不知道在說哪一位女士。

🔊 Books <u>which</u> have beautiful covers can attract readers' attention.

有著漂亮封面的書籍可以吸引讀者的注意。

Books 是什麼書並沒有說清楚，需要用 which have beautiful

covers 來補充說明，指一片書海中唯有封面設計出色的書才能吸引讀者的注意。

b. 非限定子句：如果 which / who 前面的名詞「已經明確指出」是什麼東西或是誰，後面的子句須用非限定子句。非限定子句的前面需要加逗點，如：

🎧 Ms. Julie Wong, <u>who</u> lives in Taichung, is an English teacher.
王茉莉小姐，住在台中，是個英文老師。

Ms. Julie Wong 是有名有姓的人物，她是英文老師也再清楚不過，who lives in Taichung 只是補充說明她住台中，省略這個子句，整句也說得通。

🎧 *The Lord of the Rings*, <u>which</u> was written by J. R. R. Tolkien, has been adapted into movies.
由托爾金撰寫的《魔戒》已改編成電影。

《魔戒》是小說名，它已改編成電影，這本小說由 Tolkien 所寫（which was written by J. R. R. Tolkien）只是補充的資料，整句話沒有它也很完整。

朗讀 CD 第 10 軌

12-1 生字 Vocabulary

 互動光碟

humid	(adj.)潮濕的
previous	(adj.)以前的
cram school	(n.)補習班
soaking wet	(ph.)濕透的、濕淋淋的
temperature	(n.)溫度
Centigrade(Celsius)	(n.)攝氏度數(Fahrenheit 華氏度數)
air conditioner	(n.)冷氣機
electricity	(n.)電
due to	(ph.)因為
energy crisis	(n.)能源危機
light bulb	(n.)電燈泡
energy-saving	(adj.)省電的
unplug	(v.)拔插頭(動詞三態 unplug, unplugged, unplugged)
electrical appliance	(n.)電器用品
assert	(v.)聲稱(動詞三態 assert, asserted, asserted)

n.＝名詞　ph.＝詞組　v.＝動詞　adv.＝副詞　adj.＝形容詞

electricity bill	(n.)電費
shopping bag	(n.)購物袋
mango	(n.)芒果
lychee	(n.)荔枝
plastic bag	(n.)塑膠袋
allow	(v.)讓（allow, allowed, allowed）
recycle	(v.)回收（名詞是 recycling）

朗讀 CD 第 11 軌

互動光碟

12-2 課文 Text

This summer vacation, which started on July 1st and ends on September 11th[1], seems to be hotter and more **humid**[2] than the **previous**[3] ones. Every day after four hours of English and math lessons at the **cram school**, my clothes are **soaking wet**. Today, the **temperature** even went up to 36 degrees **Centigrade**[3]. Mom, however, banned us from using **air conditioners**[4]. Her reason is that we have to save **electricity** in our house **due to**[5] the recent **energy crisis**.

What she did to save energy was, first, to change all of our **light bulbs** to the **energy-saving** ones. She then **unplugged**[6] all of the **electrical appliances** which were not in use[7], **asserting** that this would reduce our **electricity bills**[8]. Whenever[9] I leave my room, even if it is only for five minutes, she reminds me to turn the light off. But the worst thing that she did was to limit our time for watching TV and playing video games!

I am now carrying a **shopping bag**[10] that my mom made to buy some **mangoes** and **lychees**. As you can probably guess, using **plastic bags** is not **allowed** in our house. I think if everyone adopted[11] the same methods that[12] are used by my "**recycling**-crazy mom," the world would be a much better place to live.

＊注意：提到自己的媽媽(Mom)或爸爸(Dad)時，第一個字母要大寫。如果前面加了所有格代名詞如 my dad, his mom，則第一個字母小寫即可。英式英文中，Mom 做 Mum。

12-3 課文翻譯

　　從七月一日放到九月十一日的今年暑假好像比過去的暑假都來得炎熱和潮濕。每天在補習班上完四小時的英文和數學課後，我的衣服都濕透了。今天，氣溫甚至高達攝氏36度，可是媽媽卻不讓我們開冷氣，她的理由是基於最近的能源危機，我們在家裡得省電。

　　她節省能源的第一步是把全部的電燈泡換成省電燈泡。接著她拔下所有沒有在用的電器插頭，堅持這樣可以節省電費。每當我離開房間時，即使只有五分鐘，她也會提醒我關燈。不過她做的事中最糟的是限制我們看電視和打電動的時間！

　　我現在正提著媽媽做的購物袋買芒果和荔枝。你也許可以猜到，在我家不准使用塑膠袋。我想如果每個人都跟我這個「瘋狂回收老媽」實行同樣方法的話，這個世界就會變得更適合人居住。

朗讀 CD 第 12 軌

 互動光碟

12-4 解析 Language Focus

1. 這句是非限定關係子句，中間這句子句 which started on July 1st and ends on September 11th 是額外增添的資訊，去掉此子句意思也很完整。

2. humid 潮濕的、悶熱的（形容詞）；humidity 濕度（名詞）

   ◎ Taiwan is very <u>humid</u> during the summer.
   台灣夏天很潮濕。

   ◎ Today's <u>humidity</u> reached 85%. No wonder I felt very uncomfortable.
   今天的濕度高達 85％，怪不得我覺得很不舒服。

3. Centigrade＝Celsius 攝氏度數。Fahrenheit 華氏度數

   攝氏1度＝華氏32度

   （華氏度數－32度）×5/9＝攝氏度數

4. air conditioner 冷氣機（指具體的機器）

   ◎ There are no <u>air conditioners</u> in our house.
   我家沒裝冷氣機。

   air conditioning 空調（指功能）

   ◎ The <u>air conditioning</u> in this room is too strong.
   這間房間的冷氣太強。

   be air conditioned 冷氣開放的

   ◎ Our school classrooms are <u>air conditioned</u>.
   我們學校教室有冷氣。

5. due to＝because of 因為，後面接名詞

6. plug 插頭（名詞）、plug in 插插頭（動詞）、unplug 拔插頭（動詞）

7. All the electrical appliances which were not in use... 這裡須用限定子句界定一下，是沒在使用的才需要拔插頭

8. electricity bill 電費，water bill 水費，phone bill 電話費，gas bill 瓦斯費

9. whenever 無論何時，whoever 不管是誰，wherever 不論在哪裡，whatever 不管什麼。以上都可用 no matter when / who / where / what 來代替

   ♪ Whenever I go to the library, he is there.
   不管我何時去圖書館，他都在那裡。（No matter when...）

   ♪ Whoever answers the question will get the prize.
   誰回答這個問題就會得到獎品。（No matter who...）

   ♪ Wherever he hides, we'll find him.（No matter where...）
   不管他藏在哪裡，我們都會找到他。

   ♪ Whatever he says, I don't believe him.（No matter what...）
   不管他說什麼，我都不信。

10. I am now carrying a shopping bag that my mom made... 這句子句是限定子句，因先行詞 a shopping bag 不是一般的購物袋，而是媽媽親手做的

11. adopt 在高級本上冊出現很多次，讀者應該記得認養（adopt）貓的情節，不過這裡的 adopt 當作「採用」的意思

12. Everyone adopted the same methods that are used by my "recycle-crazy mom", ...

   關係子句 that are used by my "recycle-crazy mom"，是限定子句，特指我媽媽的方法

12-5-1 選選看

1. The woman _____ name is Julie is on the phone.
   (a) whose (b) which (c) what

2. The man _____ you met in the gym(體育館) is my dentist.
   (a) whom (b) whose (c) where

3. He told me about a student _____ has taken TOEFL (考托福) ten times.
   (a) which (b) whom (c) who

4. The waitress _____ I talked to is very patient.
   (a) what (b) whom (c) where

5. I am looking for a community school _____ offers computer courses.
   (a) what (b) that (c) in which

6. The class _____ I did well in high school was math.
   (a) in which (b) in what (c) in where

7. The swimming pool(游泳池) _____ we swim every day is very clean.
   (a) in which (b) at which (c) on which

8. I have no idea _____ she will show up.
   (a) when (b) who (c) which

9. They wondered _____ much they will charge us.
   (a) what (b) so (c) how

10. _____ happens, keep calm.
    (a) Whoever (b) Whatever (c) Whichever

11. The water _____ I drank last night tasted awful.

　　(a) what　(b) that　(c) with which

12. Do you remember the day _____ we first met?

　　(a) where　(b) with whom　(c) when

13. Jane can't come to the party, _____ is a pity（可惜）.

　　(a) what　(b) which　(c) how

14. I don't know the girl with _____ you were talking.

　　(a) that　(b) who　(c) whom

15. Taipei, _____ has an MRT（捷運）system, is a very convenient place to live.

　　(a) which　(b) what　(c) that

16. Yesterday we visited the Science Museum, _____ I had never visited before.

　　(a) where　(b) which　(c) what

17. The *Harry Potter* book series, _____ interests children of all ages, sells very well in Taiwan.

　　(a) that　(b) which　(c) what　（＊注意 a series of books 是一套書，是單數，後面動詞要加 s）

18. I don't like horror movies _____ have ghosts in them.

　　(a) that　(b) what　(c) when

19. I stay in Peter's apartment _____ I visit New York.

　　(a) whoever　(b) whatever　(c) whenever

20. The energy-saving light bulbs _____ were bought by Mom are in the bag.

　　(a) that　(b) what　(c) in which

21. Mom asked me to turn the light off _____ I left my room.

　　(a) where　(b) when　(c) that

22. The air conditioner _____ was bought five years ago is broken.

　　(a) which　(b) about which　(c) in which

23. I don't know _____ made that beautiful shopping bag.

　　(a) when　(b) who　(c) what

24. Which was the movie _____ you saw yesterday?

　　(a) which　(b) what　(c) that

25. I like people _____ smile a lot.

　　(a) whom　(b) which　(c) who

12-5-2 填填看

which, where, why, when, who, how, what,
with which, whether, that, in which, with whom, whose

1. I am not sure _____ the restaurant is.
2. We are wondering _____ he will come to the party or not.
3. I don't think _____ he said is true.
4. The China Post, _____ was the first English newspaper in Taiwan, used to be very popular.
5. Henry, _____ is as tall as a basketball player, can't play ball at all.
6. She found a tool _____ she could fix her broken clock.
7. This is the most interesting book _____ I have ever read.
8. Is that the girl _____ you live?
9. Can you find a girl _____ name is Meili?
10. This is the apartment _____ my boss is living.
11. They can't decide _____ would be the best time to sell their stocks (賣股票).
12. I don't know the reason _____ he has kept the secret for so long.
13. We all want to know _____ she managed to save so much money.
14. He quit smoking, _____ was a big surprise.
15. I just met Peter, _____ wife teaches at Feng Chia University.

12-5-3 問答

1. When did the writer's summer vacation start?

_____

2.   When will his summer vacation end?

_____

3.   How is the weather this summer?

_____

4.   What does the writer do every day during the summer vacation?

_____

5.   Why did his mom ban them from using the air conditioner?

_____

6.   What kind of light bulbs do they use?

_____

7.   Why did his mom unplug the electrical appliances?

_____

8.   Whenever the writer leaves his room, what does his mom remind him to do?

_____

9.   When the writer shopped for fruit, what did he carry with him?

_____

10. What are not allowed to be used in the writer's house?

_____

11. What kind of fruit is the writer going to buy?

_____

12. What kind of nickname（綽號）did the writer give to his mom?

_____

12-5-4 改錯

1.   I don't like the boy with who you danced.
2.   Please tell me that you did last night.
3.   Peter is the person who he was talking to me in the library.
4.   This is the town when I was born.

5. I found the bike that you are looking for it.

6. The house which we live is very comfortable.

7. I will never forget the day which I met you.

8. I enjoyed the trip that I took it last week.

9. Amy was the last person whom arrived today.

10. The trip was quite interesting that I took last week.

11. I am not sure where does he live.

12. The woman about who you were talking is right over there.

13. This is Henry, whom you met him last night.

14. The Taipei Times, the newspaper that you buy it every day, is hiring new reporters.

15. Please tell me where is the ladies' room.

16. I don't know when is he going to leave.

17. You need to find out who is he first.

18. The person who we met him at Tina's party called me today.

19. The book is very interesting which you lent to me.

20. The building in that my dad works is on Sanmin Road.

12-5-5 請將兩句合為一句 (用關係子句)：

1. This is Cindy. You met her last week.

   例句：This is Cindy, whom you met last week.

2. I found the textbook. You are looking for the textbook.

   _____

3. He wrote a novel. The novel's name is *Accidental Encounter*.

   _____

4. I am carrying a shopping bag. The shopping bag was made by my mom.

   _____

5. He is riding a bike. The bike is very expensive.

    _____

6. A man answered the phone. His voice is very deep.

    _____

7. A nurse helped us. She was very patient.

    _____

8. We know a lot of people. They live in Taitung.

    _____

9. Do you know the girl? John is talking to the girl.

    _____

10. I gave her all the money. The money is all I had.

    _____

11. Peter's soup is too salty. The soup is in the fridge(冰箱).

    _____

12. Your mom called this morning. She will call again tonight.

    _____

12-5-6 英文該怎麼寫？

1. 住在你家隔壁的女士是我的英文老師。(The woman...)

    _____

2. 你找到你遺失的摩托車了嗎？(Have you found...)

    _____

3. 這是我看過最糟的一部電影。(This is...)

    _____

4. 你上星期買的科幻小說很有趣。(The science-fiction...)

    _____

5. 這是我爸爸剛買的冷氣。(This is...)

_____

6. 我從七月三號放到六號的假期不太長。(My vacation...)

_____

7. 我讀的這家補習班很受歡迎。(The cram school...)

_____

8. 因為能源危機，所有東西都變貴了。(Due to...)

_____

9. 當我正在用電腦時請不要拔插頭。(When...)

_____

10. 我媽媽不讓我用塑膠袋。(My mom doesn't...)

_____

11. 我昨天買的這本小說很有趣。(The novel...)

_____

12. 這家百貨公司送的(gave away)購物袋很大。(The shopping bags...)

_____

第十三課 Unit 13

省略 who/whom/that/which 的關係子句

　　上一課我們花了許多篇幅講解子句的結構與型態，以及子句中經常使用的關係子句，但一般英文文章裡所出現的關係子句中的關鍵字──關係代名詞，如 who, whom, that 和 which 卻常常可以省略不用，如：

- The address (that) he gave me was incorrect.
  他給我的這個地址不對。

- The man (who is) riding a foldable bike is my colleague.
  騎小摺的是我的同事。

- The police (who were) led by dogs captured the criminal.
  由狗帶路的警察抓到了犯人。

　　不過，有些子句中的關係代名詞卻不能省略，如果拿掉了這幾個關鍵字，整句的意思就不清楚了。例如：

- The woman <u>who</u> lives across from us is a novelist.
  住在我們對面的女士是位小說家。

*注意：這句<u>不能去掉關係代名詞</u> who 而改寫成 ~~The woman lives across from us is a novelist.~~

- This is the key <u>that</u> opens my office.
  這是開我辦公室的鑰匙。

*注意：這句不能去掉關係代名詞 that 而改寫成 ~~This is the key opens my office.~~

　　接著我們再來看一則報上刊登的新聞片段：

A college student promised a trip to Japan by his parents if he quit playing online games for three months decided he would rather play games than travel.

　　這個句子省略了關係代名詞 who 和它後面的 be 動詞，所以讓人看了一頭霧水，不知哪一個動詞是主要句子的動詞？而哪一個動詞是子句的動詞？哪一個看似過去式卻是過去分詞？現在我們再把這個句子原來的句型還原，並把子句用括弧標明出來，讀者試試看能否翻譯出這個複雜的句型：

A college student (who was promised a trip to Japan by his parents if he quit playing online games for three months) decided that he would rather play games than travel.

　　中文翻譯：

　　一個被爸媽允諾如果戒電玩三個月就讓他去日本旅遊的大學生決定寧可打電玩，也不想去旅行。

　　看了上面幾個例句，讀者一定會想：什麼時候可以把 who, whom, that 和 which 拿掉？什麼時候又非得保留 who, whom, that 和 which 呢？現在將子句中可以省略關係代名詞的情形條列於後：

I. 介系詞前的關係代名詞和 be 動詞可以省略，例如：

　　🎧 A client (who is) from Belgium speaks five languages.
　　　有一位從比利時來的客戶會說五種語言。

　　🎧 The girl (who is) at the computer is my sister.
　　　在電腦前的女孩是我的妹妹。

II. 關係代名詞 who / whom / that / which 當作受詞時，可以省略，
　　例如：

　　🎧 Are these the keys (that) you were looking for?
　　　這些是你在找的鑰匙嗎？（這些鑰匙是(被)你找的，that＝the keys，that 是 were looking for 的受詞，可以省略。）

🎧 The engineers〔whom〕you met last night are very professional.
昨晚你見到的那些工程師非常專業。(工程師是(被)你見到的,whom=the engineers,所以 whom 是 met 的受詞,可以省略。)

III. 關係代名詞 who / whom / that / which 當作主詞時,可以省略,不過要將子句中的主要動詞改為動詞+ing,例如:

🎧 Do you know the people who live next door?
＝Do you know the people living next door?
你認識住在隔壁的人嗎?(who＝the people 當作主詞。)

🎧 The dog that barked loudly scared me.
＝The dog barking loudly scared me.
這隻大聲吠叫的狗把我嚇到了。(that＝the dog 當作主詞。)

IV. 關係代名詞當作主詞,而該子句的主要動詞是進行式時,關係代名詞 who / that / which 和它後面的 be 動詞都可以省略,例如:

🎧 The woman who is talking to John is his boss.
＝The woman talking to John is his boss.
正在跟約翰說話的女士是他的老闆。(who=the woman,在子句中當主詞用。)

🎧 The cat that was climbing up the tree is Peter's.
＝The cat climbing up the tree is Peter's.
正爬上樹的貓是彼得的。

V. 子句中主要動詞是被動時,關係代名詞 who / that / which 和它後面的 be 動詞都可以省略,例如:

🎧 The boy who was chosen to be class leader is my cousin.
＝The boy chosen to be class leader is my cousin.

這位被選為班長的男孩是我的表弟。

🎵 The houses <u>which were designed</u> by her are inexpensive.

＝The houses <u>designed</u> by her are inexpensive.

這些她設計的房子都不貴。

VI. 非限定關係子句的關係代名詞和 be 動詞可以省略：

🎵 Mr. Yang, <u>who is</u> my English teacher, will retire this year.

Mr. Yang, my English teacher, will retire this year.

我的英文老師楊先生今年退休。

🎵 My bike, <u>which was</u> stolen last night, is a mountain bike.

My bike, stolen last night, is a mountain bike.

我昨晚被偷的腳踏車是台登山越野車。

VII. when 和 why 用在<u>限定關係子句</u>時可以省略，但是 where 則不能省略，如以下兩句中的 when 和 why 都可以省略：

🎵 January is a month（when）people like to stay at home.

一月是一般人喜歡待在家裡的月份。

🎵 I would like to know the reason（why）he couldn't come.

我想知道他不能來的理由。

可是 where 在<u>限定關係子句</u>和<u>非限定關係子句</u>都不能省略，如：

🎵 非限定：She likes to visit Japan, <u>where</u> she can go to hot springs.

她喜歡去日本，在那裡她可以泡湯。

🎵 限定：She likes to visit places <u>where</u> she can totally relax.

她喜歡去讓她可以徹底放鬆的地方。（口語常省略 where，但書寫時 where 多保留。）

朗讀 CD 第 13 軌

13-1 生字 Vocabulary

互動光碟

rigorous	(adj.)難的，嚴格的
written test	(ph.)筆試
driving test	(ph.)路考
driver's license	(ph.)駕照
test drive	(ph.)試開
dent	(n.)使凹下(dent, dented, dented)
block	(n.)街區
public transportation	(ph.)大眾交通工具
challenge	(v.)挑戰(challenge, challenged, challenged)
retort	(v.)回嘴、反駁(retort, retorted, retorted)
master	(v.)精通、熟練(master, mastered, mastered)
grocery	(n.)食品雜貨
lay	(v.)放置(lay, laid, laid)
heroine	(n.)女主角

n.＝名詞　ph.＝詞組　v.＝動詞　adv.＝副詞　adj.＝形容詞

announce	(v.)宣布(announce, announced, announced)
guy	(n.)人
nevertheless	(adv.)儘管如此
schedule	(v. n.)把……列入計畫或時間表；日程表(名詞)

朗讀 CD 第 14 軌

互動光碟

13-2 課文 Text

Good news! After **rigorous written** and **driving tests**[1], Mom got the **driver's license** (that) she had long been dreaming of[2]. Yesterday, she took her first **test drive**. It was quite successful; at least, she returned without **denting** the car. Today, as she was about to[3] drive to the supermarket (which is) a few **blocks**[4] from our home, Dad stopped her and asked her, "Aren't you the person who always makes[5] us ride bikes or take **public transportation**[6]?"

Challenged[7] by Dad, Mom **retorted**, "I need more practice to **master** my driving skills." Two hours later, Mom, (who was) wearing[8] a confident smile on her face, came back with the **groceries**. Before **laying**[9] the bags carefully down on the floor, our **heroine**[10] **announced**: "I will drive you **guys** to Puli to see Grandma!"

Dad, (who was[11]) just getting ready to leave the city for some fresh air, took out his mountain bike and said happily, "I guess we can all take our bikes to Puli and ride around that beautiful town." I didn't really want to be home alone; **nevertheless**, worried[12] about the final exam, (which is) **scheduled** for the twenty-first of June, I decided to stay at home and study.

13-3 課文翻譯

　　好消息！經過嚴格的筆試和路考後，媽媽拿到她一直夢寐以求的駕照。昨天她第一次試開，開得還蠻成功的，至少回來時車子沒有坑坑巴巴的。今天，她正準備開車到離我家幾條街區外的超級市場時，爸爸把她攔下來問道：「妳不是老是逼我們騎腳踏車和搭大眾交通工具嗎？」

　　被爸爸一質疑，媽媽反駁：「我需要多練習才能熟悉開車技術。」兩小時後，臉上掛著一抹自信笑容的媽滿載而歸。把袋子小心放在地上之前，這位女中豪傑宣布：「我開車載你們去埔里看阿嬤！」

　　正準備離開城市到郊外呼吸新鮮空氣的爸爸，抬出他的登山越野車，開心地說：「我想我們可以開車載著腳踏車，繞著美麗的小鎮騎一圈。」我很不想獨自一人在家，不過，擔心著六月二十一日舉行的期末段考，我決定還是待在家裡讀書。

朗讀 CD 第 15 軌 **13-4 解析 Language Focus**

 互動光碟

1. take a written test 考筆試，take an oral test 考口試，take a driving test 考路考

2. 用關係代名詞合併句子

Mom got <u>the driver's license</u>.

Mom had been dreaming of <u>the driver's license</u> for a long time.

兩句都提到 the driver's license，可以合併為一句：

Mom got the driver's license <u>that</u> she had been dreaming of for a long time.

我們現在再看一個較簡單的例子：

She bought a <u>handbag</u>.
她買了一個皮包。

The <u>handbag</u> is expensive.
這個皮包很貴。

→ She bought a handbag <u>which</u> is expensive. 或者
The handbag (which) she bought is expensive.
她買了一個很貴的皮包。

She bought a <u>handbag</u>.
她買了一個皮包。

She likes the <u>handbag</u> very much.
她很喜歡這個皮包。

→ She bought a handbag <u>that</u> she likes very much.
她買了一個她很喜歡的皮包。

3. be about to 事情立刻即將發生。be going to 事情將發生

4. block 可以當名詞用，表「街區」，例如：

   ✎ We live on the same block.
   我們住在同一街區。

   也可以當動詞用，表「封鎖」，例如：

   ✎ The road was blocked off by the police.
   這條街被警察封鎖了。

5. make, have, let 是使役動詞，後面的動詞用原形，例如：

   ✎ He often makes me laugh.
   他常讓我大笑。

   ✎ They won't let me go.
   他們不讓我走。

   ✎ She seldom has her boyfriend pay for her.
   她很少要她男友幫她付錢。

   如果使役動詞後面的動詞有被動的意味，要接動詞的第三態變化，例如：

   ✎ I had my car fixed.
   我請人幫我修車。

   ✎ She had her hair cut.
   她請人幫她剪髮。

6. public transportation system 大眾捷運系統，包括公車（bus）、地鐵（metro, underground, subway）、火車（train）、有軌電車（tram），至於我們的捷運 MRT 則是 Mass Rapid Transit 的簡寫

7. 用分詞構句合併句子

   Mom was challenged by Dad.

   Mom retorted, "I need more practice."

   兩句主詞都是 Mom，可以合併為：

Mom, (who was) challenged by Dad, retorted, "I need more practice."

也可以改為 Challenged by Dad, Mom retorted, "I need more practice."

8. 英文詞彙中動詞與名詞的搭配很有學問，不能用中文直接翻譯，如 wear 這個字，常用來搭配的名詞有：

- wear a mustache 留短髭
- wear a beard 留鬍子
- wear long hair 留長髮
- wear a smile 掛著微笑

9. 下面三組動詞及其三態變化很容易混淆：

lie, lay, lain, lying 躺

I can lie down and quickly fall asleep.

我可以躺下很快就睡著。

lay, laid, laid, laying 放

He laid his report on the teacher's desk.

他把報告放在老師桌上。

lie, lied, lied, lying 說謊

He lied about his age.

他虛報年齡。

10. heroine 原意是書中的女主角，男主角是 hero，不過 heroine 亦可指「女英雄，女傑」，這裡則指母親很勇敢。My heroine 是指我佩服的女人。

11. 這句是非限定關係子句，關係代名詞和 be 動詞可省略。

12. 用分詞構句合併句子

I was worried about the final exam.

I decided to stay at home and study.

這兩句的主詞都是 I，我們可以把它們合為一句：

Worried about the final exam, I decided to stay at home and study.

13-5-1 選選看

請看下列句子中的關係代名詞可以省略不用嗎？如果可以省略也可以不省略，請在空格中寫(a/b)，如果絕對不能省略，請寫(a)

1. She has a cat _____ named Mumu.
   (a) which is　(b) X

2. Students _____ fail the entrance exam can try again.
   (a) who　(b) X

3. The magazine _____ covers(報導)bikes made in Taiwan is mine.
   (a) that　(b) X

4. The man _____ is angry is my math teacher.
   (a) who　(b) X

5. Mom has taken written and driving tests, _____ were both very difficult.
   (a) which　(b) X

6. I went to the supermarket _____ a few blocks away from my apartment.
   (a) that is　(b) X

7. The woman _____ car broke down is making a phone call.
   (a) whose　(b) X

8. The hall(大廳) _____ her wedding will be held has been cleaned.
   (a) in which　(b) X

9. What's the name of that person _____ first walked on the moon?
   (a) who　(b) X

10. I like the black tea _____ sent by her from India(印度).

    (a) that was   (b) X

11. She doesn't like cheese, _____ is different from me.

    (a) which   (b) X

12. This is Ms. Lee, _____ we met at the convenience store the other day(那天).

    (a) whom   (b) X

13. We cannot meet the writer today, _____ is a pity(真可惜).

    (a) which   (b) X

14. The writer _____ you saw at the bookstore is Jiou Ba Dau.

    (a) whom   (b) X

15. Do you know the girl _____ talking to Tom?

    (a) who is   (b) X

16. I told you about the woman _____ lives next door.

    (a) who   (b) X

17. Do you see the cat _____ lying on the sofa?

    (a) that is   (b) X

18. Tom, _____ our class leader, failed the final exam(期末考).

    (a) who is   (b) X

19. Peter has an Iranian friend(伊朗的朋友)_____ he met on the Internet.

    (a) whom   (b) X

20. Amy, _____ excited about tomorrow's trip, cannot sleep.

    (a) who is   (b) X

13-5-2 合併句子

請將兩句合併為一句，並將關係代名詞或其後面的 be 動詞省略

1. Do you know the boy?

   We met a boy yesterday?

   Do you know _____

2. I don't like the table.

   My parents bought the table yesterday.

   I don't like _____

3. The apples are sweet.

   The apples are laid on the table.

   The apples _____

4. Do you know the girl?

   The girl is riding on the bike with Tom.

   Do you know _____

5. Peter is very nice.

   We met Peter yesterday.

   Peter, the person _____

6. I told you about the woman.

   The woman is living next door.

   I told you _____

7. The bank is near my apartment.

   The bank was robbed last week.(銀行被搶)

   The bank _____

8. Jane's mom was a musician(音樂家).

   Jane's mom passed away last night.

   Jane's mom, _____

9. The temple is very old.

We visited the temple last night.

The temple _____

10. We went to Seoul last month.

Seoul is the capital of Korea.

We went to Seoul, _____

13-5-3問答

1. Before the writer's got her driver's license, what kinds of tests did she have to pass（通過）?

_____

2. How was the writer's mom's first test driving test?

_____

3. Where was the writer's mom going to drive to today?

_____

4. Where is the supermarket the writer's mom was going to drive to?

_____

5. Why did the writer's dad stop his mom before she drove to the supermarket?

_____

6. When the writer's mom was challenged by his dad, what did she say?

_____

7. How long did it take the writer's mom to shop for groceries?

It took her _____

8. Where did Mom plan to drive?

_____

9. How did the writer's dad react to his mom's announcement?

_____

10. Did the writer go to Puli with his parents?

_____

11. Why did the writer decide to stay at home?

_____

13-5-4 改錯

1. This is the convenience store(便利商店) sells cheap sushi(壽司).
2. The temple I visited it last weekend is very old.
3. The day I arrive was very warm.
4. Is he the boy lives next door?
5. Bob, interesting in music, decided to become a musician.
6. Ms. Lin, who very smart, lives on the corner of the street.
7. The man ate 30 hamburgers in an hour died.
8. He is the man you called him last night.
9. She always likes to stay in a hotel she can swim.
10. Summer is the time I swimming a lot.

13-5-5英文該怎麼寫？

1. 今天下午我考(took)的期末段考真難。(The final exam...)

_____

2. 他不知道我留在家裡的原因。(He doesn't know...)

_____

3. 下星期我會開車載你們去埔里，那裡是我阿嬤住的地方。(Next week I will...)

_____

4. 我媽媽買回來的東西很重。(The groceries...)

_____

5. 這家離我家幾個街區的超級市場很大。(The supermarket...)

   _____

6. 這台我父母去年夏天買的冷氣機壞了 (is broken)。(The air conditioner...)

   _____

7. 我喜歡的溫度是攝氏20度。(The temperature...)

   _____

8. 這個我媽媽做的購物袋很漂亮。(The shopping bag...)

   _____

9. 現在當令(in season)的芒果和荔枝很便宜。(Mangoes and lychees,...)

   _____

10. 臉上掛著自信笑容的那個女孩是我們的班長。(That girl wearing...)

   _____

第十四課 Unit 14

假設法

互動光碟

　　我們常常在談話中會用到「如果」起頭的條件子句，例如：「如果需要幫忙，請跟我聯絡。If you need any help, please contact me.」、「如果他能來，我們都會很高興。If he can come, we will be happy.」、「如果我是你的話，我不會去見他。If I were you, I would not meet him tomorrow.」「如果上星期她在這裡的話，當時情況就會大不相同。If she had been here last week, the situation would have been very different.」以上這些句子雖然都用「如果」開頭，句子中的含義卻不同，有的是平鋪直述的事實、有的是與事實相反的假設、有的時間點設在現在，有的卻設在過去(如果當時他……)，有的結果在當下就看到了、有的卻會在不久的將來才看到結果。

　　條件子句是由兩個句子組合而成：一為設定一個條件(if you don't eat)，一為造成的結果(you will be hungry)。或是一為假設一個狀況(if I were Michael Jackson)，一為在那個狀況下的反應(I would want my old face back.)，兩句中間用逗點相連：If you don't eat, you will be hungry. 這句也可寫成：You will be hungry if you don't eat.(＊注意：if子句放在句尾時，中間不用逗點隔開。)

　　由上面兩個例子可知條件子句依其敘事的內容可分為兩種：事實(真實的、可能會發生的)和非事實(不真實的、不可能發生的、假想的、與事實相反的)。現在我們將這個看似簡單，其實卻很複雜的句型分類詳述於後：

I. 眞實的條件子句

1. 不變的事實：例如：

> If you heat butter, it melts.
> 你把奶油加熱，它就會融化。

2. 接命令句的條件子句：

🐦 If you call her, please tell her to contact me.
如果你打電話給她，請叫她跟我聯絡。（Do your homework.
做功課、Take a shower. 洗澡、Please help me move this. 請幫
我搬開這個。都是命令句。）

3. 未來會發生的事實：

🐦 If I see Peter, I will tell him.（see 用現在式，tell 用未來式。）
如果我看到 Peter，我會告訴他。

🐦 If I have extra money, I will save it.
如果我有餘錢，我將會存起來。

🐦 If it rains tomorrow, we will still go.
如果明天下雨的話，我們還是會去。

＊注意：雖然指明天下雨，if 子句中的 rain 仍用現在式。另外 will 也可
以用其他助動詞，如 may, might, should, can 代替。如：

🐦 If it rains tomorrow, we may stay at home.
如果明天下雨，我們可能待在家裡。

4. 發生在過去的事實：

🐦 If he didn't come to the class yesterday, he must be ill.
如果他昨天沒來上課，他一定是病了。

II. 與事實相反的條件子句

1. 與現在事實相反的假設：

🐦 If I now had one million dollars, I would study abroad.
如果我現在有一百萬的話，我會出國留學。（事實是你現在
沒有一百萬，也沒辦法出國，以上的句子只是你的夢想。）

＊注意：與現在事實相反的假設語氣用過去式（had、would stay）來與「真正發生」的現在（簡單）式做出區隔，句中用的雖是過去式，但表達的卻是現在假想的一件事。I would study abroad. 可以縮寫為 I'd study abroad.

◎ If I <u>were</u> the Minister of Education, I <u>would cancel</u> all the exams.
如果我是教育部長的話，我會廢除所有的考試。（你不是教長，但你可以假設自己是教長。）

＊注意：如果用假設語氣 I, she, he, it, we 後面接的 be 動詞都用 <u>were</u>，不用 was。）

◎ If you <u>asked</u> him now, he <u>would help</u> you.
假如你現在問他，他一定會幫你。（事實是你還沒開口，他當然不能幫你。）

＊注意：這句雖然用的是過去式，但實際上是發生在當下的一個情況。

2. 發生在<u>過去</u>與過去事實相反的假設：

◎ If he <u>had taken</u> that bus yesterday, he <u>might have been killed</u> in the accident.
如果他昨天搭上這班（死亡）巴士，他也許會死於這場車禍。（事實是：He didn't take the bus. 他沒搭上這班車。）

◎ If I <u>had read</u> the book, I <u>would have understood</u> what he said.
如果我當時讀了這本書的話，我（當時）會瞭解他說的話。（事實是：I didn't read that book, so I didn't understand what he said at that time.）

◎ If I <u>had read</u> the book, I <u>would understand</u> what he is saying.
如果我當時讀了這本書的話，我（現在）會瞭解他說的話。

III. if 當做「是否」用：

與條件子句無關，if 還有一種常用的句型，用在不確定的狀況時，例如：

- I wonder <u>if</u> my English teacher will let me pass the course.
  我不知道英文老師會不會讓我過。

- I don't know <u>if</u> he will stay here over night.
  我不知道他會不會留在這裡過夜。

- They asked me <u>if</u> I would teach them next semester.
  他們問我下學期是否會教他們。

  * 注意：以上句子中的 if 也可以用 whether 取代，後面可加 or not，亦可省略。

- I wonder <u>whether</u> my English teacher will let me pass (or not).
  I don't know <u>whether</u> he will stay here over night (or not).
  They asked me <u>whether</u> I would teach them next semester (or not).

IV. 假設語氣中 wish 的用法：

1. 現在式

- It's hot. I wish I <u>were</u> in Iceland right now.
  真熱，我希望我現在在冰島。(事實是 You are in Taiwan right now.)

  * 注意：假設語氣的 be 動詞都用 were。

- She wishes her boyfriend <u>liked</u> swimming.
  她希望她的男友喜歡游泳。(事實是 Her boyfriend doesn't like swimming.)

2. 過去式

🎵 I wish I had learned Japanese when I was in college.

我希望大學時學了日文。(事實是 I didn't learn Japanese when I was in college.)

🎵 He wishes she had seen the movie with him yesterday.

他希望她昨天跟他去看了電影。(事實是 She didn't see the movie with him yesterday.)

3. 未來式

🎵 I wish he could stop playing computer games.

我希望他可以戒掉電玩。(事實是 He can't stop playing.)

🎵 He wishes she would help him.

他希望她會幫他。(事實是 She won't help him.)

* 注意 hope 和 wish 都有希望的意思，但用法有時相同，有時卻不同，如我希望再見到你，這句話可以用 wish，也可以用 hope：

🎵 I wish to see you again.

🎵 I hope to see you again.

但 hope 和 wish 也有不同的地方：

表達單純的希望用 hope，如：

🎵 I hope you can come to the party next week.

我希望你下星期能來派對。

表達與事實相反的願望，或表達不滿時用 wish，如：

🎵 I wish he could be quiet.

我希望你能安靜一點。

* 注意：wish 表達與事實相反的願望，後面用過去式 could。

朗讀 CD 第 16 軌

互動光碟

14-1 生字 Vocabulary

get some sun	(ph.)曬曬太陽
lobster	(n.)龍蝦
peel	(v., n)脫皮(動詞)(peel, peeled, peeled, peeling);皮(名詞)
sunscreen	(n.)防曬油
horrible	(adj.)可怕、恐怖
flunk	(v.)當掉(flunk, flunked, flunked)
score	(n.)分數
grade report	(ph.)成績單
untouched	(adj.)沒動過的
stare at	(ph.)盯著看
sternly	(adv.)嚴肅地
bury	(v.)埋(bury, buried, buried)
current events	(ph.)時事
lack	(n., v.)缺少(名詞、動詞)(lack, lacked, lacked)
according to	(ph.)根據、依照

n.＝名詞　ph.＝詞組　v.＝動詞　adv.＝副詞　adj.＝形容詞

guard	(n.)警衛
distribute	(v.)分發（distribute, distributed, distributed）
household	(n.)家庭、戶
apartment building	(ph.)公寓大樓
subscribe to	(ph.)訂閱

朗讀 CD 第 17 軌

互動光碟

14-2 課文 Text

Mom and Dad came home a week later. They **had** both **gotten some sun**, but Dad's face was as red as a cooked[1] **lobster**. Even worse, it had started **peeling**[2]. Mom kept nagging him, saying[3], "If you had put on some **sunscreen**[4], your face would not look so **horrible**[5]."

I am glad I didn't go with them. If I had gone, I might have **flunked** that important exam[6]. I thought Mom would be happy to see that I got a good **score** on the test, but as I proudly showed the **grade report** to her, she noticed a pile of **untouched** newspapers lying[7] in the corner of the living room.

She **stared at** me and said **sternly**, "If I were you, I would not just **bury** my nose in textbooks[8]." I knew that she wished I had read those newspapers and learned about some **current events**. When it comes to a **lack**[9] of interest in reading newspapers, I am not alone. **According to** the **guard** who **distributes** papers[10] in our building, only 7 out of the 120 **households**[11] in our **apartment building subscribe to** newspapers. Mom continued, "If people don't read newspapers, sooner or later, all newspapers will either go online or disappear altogether[12]."

14-3 課文翻譯

　　一星期之後爸媽回家了，他們倆都曬了太陽，但爸爸的臉紅得像隻煮熟的龍蝦，更糟糕的是，他的臉開始脫皮。媽媽不斷碎碎唸：「如果你當時塗了防曬油，你的臉現在也不至於會看起來這麼可怕。」

　　我很高興沒跟他們去。如果我去的話，那個重要的考試可能會當掉。我想媽一定很高興看到我考試成績不錯，但當我得意洋洋地把成績單給她看時，她注意到客廳角落裡放著一堆動也沒動過的報紙。

　　她瞪著我兇巴巴地說：「如果我是你的話，我不會只埋首在教科書裡。」我知道她希望我每天讀報，知道一些時事。說到不愛看報，不是只有我不看。據我們這棟樓送報的警衛說，我們這棟公寓大樓共 120 戶人家，其中只有 7 家訂報。媽接著說：「如果大家都不看報，所有的報紙遲早不是上了網，就是全都消失得無影無蹤。」

朗讀 CD 第 18 軌

14-4 解析 Language Focus

 互動光碟

1.　cooked (被)煮熟的，uncooked＝raw 生的

2.　這裡用過去完成式，指爸爸在回家(過去式)之前臉就開始脫皮了。 start 和 begin 一樣，後面可以接 to+V，也可以接 V+ing。

3.　這句也可寫成 Mom kept nagging and said...

4.　Sunscreen＝sunscreen lotion

5.　If you had put on some sunscreen, your face would not look so horrible.

　　這句請看前面說明 II 與事實相反的條件子句中 2 發生在過去與過去事實相反的假設第三句的解釋。

6.　If I had gone, I might have flunked that important exam.

　　這句請看前面說明 II 與事實相反的條件子句中 2 發生在過去與過去事實相反的假設第一和二句的解釋。

7.　lie, lay, lain, lying

　　指東西放在某個地方，如：

🔟 The plates lay on the table.
　　碟子放在桌上。

　　也指人躺在某處，如：

🔟 He lay down on the sofa.
　　他躺在沙發上。

　　也有位在某處的意思，如：

🔟 The island lies at the end of the river.
　　這個島位在河的尾端。

8. If I <u>were</u> you, I <u>wouldn't just bury</u> my head in textbooks.

這句請看前面說明 II 與事實相反的條件子句中 1 與現在事實相反的假設。媽媽引號說的中的話要用現在式,這句是現在式的假設句,be 動詞都用 were。

9. lack 可以當名詞,也可以當動詞,但要注意 lack 當動詞時後面不能加 of,如:

　　◎ Her <u>lack</u> of patience is her biggest problem.
　　　 缺乏耐心是她最大的問題。

　　◎ She <u>lacks</u> patience in dealing with children.
　　　 她沒有耐心跟小孩打交道。

10. paper 當「紙張」時,是不可數名詞,如果要可數,可以說 two sheets of paper 兩張紙。注意這裡的 papers 有加 s,是指 newspapers

11. a household name 家喻戶曉,如

　　◎ Jay Chou, a household name, is a famous Taiwanese singer.
　　　 台灣知名歌手周杰倫的名字家喻戶曉。

household chores 家事

　　◎ Boys, like girls, should do household chores.
　　　 男孩跟女孩一樣,都應該做家事。

12. all together 和 altogether 常會弄混,all together 是「在一起」,altogether 是「總合,完全地」。如:

　　◎ When was the last time we were <u>all together</u>?
　　　 上回我們聚在一起是什麼時候?

　　◎ <u>Altogether</u>, there are 145 people in the room.
　　　 全部共有 145 人在這間房裡。

　　◎ We were not <u>altogether</u> sure what was going to happen.
　　　 我們不完全知道會發生什麼事情。

14-5-1 選選看

1. If my husband _____ the cooking, I will do the dishes.
   (a) do　(b) does　(c) done

2. His mom will be very happy if he _____ the newspaper every day.
   (a) read　(b) will read　(c) reads

3. If my parents _____ in Taichung, I would live at home instead of the dorm (宿舍).
   (a) live　(b) lived　(c) living

4. If you see Amy tonight, _____ her to call me.
   (a) ask　(b) asks　(c) will ask

5. Please _____ me clean my room if you have time this afternoon.
   (a) helps　(b) helped　(c) help

6. If my mom learns about this, I _____ in trouble.
   (a) were　(b) will be　(c) would be

7. I would tell you if I _____ her name.
   (a) know　(b) knew　(c) knows

8. If I _____ to someone's house for dinner, I usually take some fruit.
   (a) go　(b) went　(c) will go

9. If I _____ many English courses when I was in college, I would speak English fluently.
   (a) take　(b) took　(c) had taken

10.　If I _____ time, I would go to the beach.
　　（a）have　（b）had　（c）has

11.　If she _____ time, she might have gone to the party.
　　（a）had　（b）have　（c）had had

12.　If you _____ to the supermarket tomorrow, will you buy some fruit for me?
　　（a）go　（b）went　（c）will go

13.　If I had gone to Puli with them, Grandma _____ very happy.
　　（a）will be　（b）would have been　（c）would had been

14. I wouldn't buy that dress if I _____ you.
　　（a）am　（b）was　（c）were

15. If you subscribed to the newspaper, you _____ about lots of current events.
　　（a）may learn　（b）would learn　（c）would have learned

14-5-2 填填看

1.　You didn't go to Puli with your parents.
　　If I _____, I would have played with my cousins.

2.　You flunked English.
　　If I hadn't flunked English, my mom wouldn't have _____ (be) so angry.

3.　It isn't raining now.
　　If it _____ (rain), I would take an umbrella（傘）or a raincoat with me.

4.　You missed a great program on TV.
　　If I _____ (come) home earlier, I might have watched that great program on TV.

5.　He didn't call her.
　　She wouldn't be so angry now if he _____ her.

6.　The newspapers were lying on the table untouched.
　　The newspapers wouldn't be lying on the table untouched if he _____ (read) them.

7. Mom has a driver's license now.

   If she didn't have a driver's license, she _____ be able to drive.

8. Many people drive cars.

   If everyone _____ (take) public transportation, the air in the city would be nicer.

9. It was hot and humid last summer.

   If it _____ so hot and humid last summer, we wouldn't have used the air conditioner that often.

10. The shopkeeper gave Dad a discount.

    If he _____ (give) Dad a discount, Mom and Dad might not have bought two bikes.

14-5-3問答

1. When did the writer's parents come home?

   _____

2. What had happened to his dad's face?

   _____

3. Why did his mom keep nagging his dad?

   _____

4. Why does the writer feel glad that he didn't go with his parents?

   _____

5. How was the writer's test result (考試成績)?

   _____

6. When the writer showed the grade report to his mom, what did she see?

   _____

7. Does his mom want him to study all the time?

   _____

8. Why does his mom hope that he will read the newspaper every day?

   _____

9. Who distributes newspapers in the writer's apartment building?

_____

10. What will happen to the newspapers if fewer and fewer people read them?

_____

14-5-4改錯

1. If I am not an only child, I would not feel so lonely and pressured.

2. Mom will not be happy if I didn't read the newspaper.

3. If I had read the newspaper, Mom won't be so upset.

4. I wish I can have another cat in addition to Inky.

5. She wishes she learned English when she was a little girl.

6. If I sell my scooter, I would buy a bike instead.

7. If she want to adopt my cat, I will give it to her.

8. If it will rain tomorrow, I will still go hiking.

9. If we went out, Mom unplugs all of the electronic appliances.

10. If you call her, you ask her to see me this afternoon.

14-5-5英文該怎麼寫

1. 如果你見到他，告訴他我正在找他。(be looking for)

_____

2. 如果當時我在那裡，我一定會很氣惱(upset)。

_____

3. 如果我現在會賺錢, 我一定會買一台腳踏車。(If I were making money...)

_____

4. 如果你擦了防曬油，你的臉現在就不會脫皮了。

_____

5. 如果明天不下雨，我會去埔里。

_____

6. 如果現在我知道她的手機號碼，我會立刻(immediately)打給她。

   _____

7. 如果當時我有數位相機的話，我一定會把那隻貓拍下來。(take a picture)

   _____

8. 如果你不帶購物袋的話，你得買塑膠袋。

   _____

9. 如果不濕熱的話，我不會開冷氣。(If it is not hot and humid...)

   _____

10. 如果他沒騎腳踏車的話，他會搭大眾交通工具(public transportation)。

   _____

第十五課 Unit 15

雖然……但是，
因為……所以

　　和「如果」一樣，我們常常在談話中也會用到「雖然……但是」和「因為……所以」的句型，但英文跟中文不一樣的是「雖然 although」和「但是 but」或「因為 because」和「所以 so」絕對不能在同一個句子裡出現，例如：「雖然他收入不高，但他常捐錢給弱勢團體。Although he doesn't have a high income, he often donates money to disadvantaged groups.」。「因為頭痛，所以今天我沒有去上學。Because I had a headache, I didn't go to school today.」。由上面的例句可看出，句子裡有了 although 就不能出現 but，有了 because 就不能出現 so。

　　英文有許多表達「雖然」的字和詞，除了 although 之外還有 though, despite, in spite of, even though, even if 和 albeit。這些字和詞的意思雖然都跟中文「雖然」、「儘管」、「即使」相當，但各自的用法有同也有異，現在將這些詞句的意思和用法，以例句說明於後：

I. although 和 though

　　although 和 though 都是連接詞，幾乎可以相互替換著用，不過 although 比 though 正式。

　　🎧　Although I like the sweater, I decided not to buy it.
　　　　雖然我喜歡這件毛衣，但我決定不買。

這句話也可寫成：

　　🎧　I decided not to buy it, although I like the sweater.
　　🎧　Though I like the sweater, I decided not to buy it.

though 可以放在句子最後面，although 卻不行。如：

　　🎧　I like the sweater. I decided not to buy it, though.

II. although 和 while

while 是「當某人在……的時候」，如：

🎵 While I was doing the dishes, he called me.
當我在洗碗時，他來電了。

while 有時也當「雖然」用，可以取代 although，如：

🎵 While I like the sweater very much, I decided not to buy it.
雖然我喜歡這件毛衣，但我決定不買。

III. even though 和 even if

even though、even if 和 though、although 的意思很像，只是比 though 和 although 語氣更強，如：

🎵 Even though I love the sweater so much, I decided not to buy it.
即便我那麼喜歡這件毛衣，我還是決定不買。

Even though 和 even if 的意思有些微的不同，even though 是陳述一個事實，通常用現在式或過去式表達；even if 則在表達假定的想法，主要子句通常用未來式表達。如：

🎵 Even though it rained heavily, they took a trip to Hualian.
即便下了大雨，他們還是去了花蓮。

🎵 Even if it rains tomorrow, they will take a trip to Hualian.
就算明天下雨，他們還是會去花蓮。

even if 有時用在與事實相反的假設語氣，如：

🎵 Even if I had time, I wouldn't go shopping.
就算我有時間，我也不會去逛街。
（事實是：今天下午我很忙，沒有時間，可是即便我有時間……）

even though 則說明真實的情況，如：

🦻 <u>Even though</u> I had time, I <u>didn't find</u> the dress I wanted.
即便我有時間，我還是找不到我想買的洋裝。
（事實是：我今天下午有時間去逛街，可是即便我有時間逛了街……）

IV. even if, even though 和 even

even 和 even if, even though 不同，它不是連接詞，而是副詞，如：

Even I read this book many times, I still couldn't understand it.（×）

🦻 <u>Even though</u> I read this book many times, I still couldn't understand it.（○）
這本書我即使讀了很多遍，還是不懂。

🦻 He works every day, <u>even</u> during Chinese New Year.（○）
他每天工作，即使春節也不例外。

🦻 He kept writing to her, <u>even</u> after she got married.（○）
他一直寫信給她，即使她婚後也不例外。

V. despite 和 in spite of 的意思用法完全一樣，它們跟 though 和 although 意思很像，不過 despite 和 in spite of 後面接名詞或動名詞，而 though 和 although 後面則接句子，如：

🦻 I couldn't sleep, <u>though</u> I was tired.
🦻 I couldn't sleep <u>despite</u> being tired.
🦻 I couldn't sleep <u>in spite of</u> being tired.
我睡不著，即使我很累。

其實 despite 和 in spite of 的後面加了 the fact that 就可以加句子，
如：

- I couldn't sleep despite the fact that I was tired.
- I couldn't sleep in spite of the fact that I was tired.

VI. although 有個比較正式的同義字「albeit」，意思與 although一
樣，通常用在書面文字，而不用在口語。如：

- The conversations with my aunt on MSN, albeit short, are such a
  joy.
  我跟阿姨在 MSN 的對話，雖短卻超好玩。

- Today's clear albeit cold weather is great for our hiking trip.
  今天天氣晴朗卻寒冷，很適合我們的健行之旅。

我們接著來談「因為」，「因為」這個詞除了可以用 because 表
達外，還可以用 because of, thanks to, due to, owing to，除了 because 接
句子外，其他後面都接名詞或動名詞。如：

- They moved to Hualian because his wife found a job there.
  他們搬到花蓮，因為他的太太在那邊找到了工作。

- They moved to Hualian because of his wife's new job.
  ＝Their moving to Hualian was due to his wife's new job.
  他們因為他太太新工作的關係而搬到花蓮。

due to 也可以放在句子最前面，如：

- Due to her illness, she can't come.
  她因病不能來。

這個句子也可以用 owing to 和 because of 取代 due to：

🎵 Owing to her illness, she can't come.

🎵 Because of her illness, she can't come.

thanks to 常接好的原因，有「多虧、幸虧」的意思，如：

🎵 Thanks to her brother's help, they could move to Hualian without any problems.

多虧她哥哥的幫忙，他們才可以順利搬到花蓮。

朗讀 CD 第 19 軌

互動光碟

15-1 生字 Vocabulary

avid	(adj.)熱心的、興趣極高的
catch a glimpse of	(ph.)瞥一眼
depress	(v.)使消沉、使沮喪(depress, depressed, depressed)
financial crisis	(ph.)金融風暴
recession	(n.)經濟不景氣
unemployment	(n.)失業、失業率
layoff	(n.)解雇
drop out of school	(n.)輟學、退學
take some odd jobs	(n.)打零工
evening news	(n.)晚間新聞
double-income	(adj.)雙薪的
closure	(n.)關閉
downsizing	(n.)精簡人事
boost consumption	(ph.)刺激消費
consumption coupon	(ph.)消費券
worth	(adj.)值

n.＝名詞　ph.＝詞組　v.＝動詞　adv.＝副詞　adj.＝形容詞

pocket money	(ph.)零用錢(英式用法)
spread	(v.)散布、蔓延(spread, spread, spread, spreading)
graduate school	(ph.)研究所
graduate	(h.)畢業生
renowned	(adj.)著名的
job hunting	(ph.)找工作
global	(adj.)全球性的

朗讀 CD 第 20 軌

互動光碟

15-2 課文 Text

Although I am not an **avid**[1] newspaper reader, once in a while, I **catch a glimpse of depressing**[2] words like "**financial crisis**," "**recession**," and "high **unemployment**[3]" in the paper. Yesterday after the ball game, Jie Ming told me about his father's recent **layoff**[4]. "Even if my parents never ask me to, I may have to **drop out of school**[5] and **take some odd jobs** to help them out," Jie Ming said sadly.

Jie Ming's family is not alone. According to the **evening news**, even some **double-income**[6] families are in trouble because of business **closures**[7] or **downsizing**. Many shops and restaurants have gone out of business despite the fact that to **boost consumption**, the government has distributed **consumption coupons worth** NT$3600 to every Taiwanese citizen[8].

Mom and Dad still give me the same amount of **pocket money** as before, but I am anxious[9] like everyone else. Anxiety is **spreading** because many college and even **graduate school graduates**[10] can't find jobs. For example, my cousin Weiren, who has a degree[11] from a **renowned** university, is still **job hunting**. I hope the **global**[12] financial crisis will be over soon.

15-3 課文翻譯

　　我雖然不太愛看報，偶爾還是會瞄到報上一些令人喪氣的字眼，如「金融風暴」、「不景氣」和「高失業率」。昨天球賽過後，傑明告訴我他父親最近被裁員的事，他很難過地說：「即使我父母沒要求我做什麼，我大概還是會休學、打些零工來幫他們。」

　　不只傑明一家，根據晚間新聞報導，連許多雙薪家庭也因為公司關門大吉或精簡人事陷入困境。儘管政府為了刺激消費，發給每個台灣公民價值台幣 3600 元的消費券，但許多店家和餐館還是歇業了。

　　雖然爸媽還是給我跟以前一樣多的零用錢，我還是跟其他人一樣憂心。而且愈來愈憂心，由於許多大學畢業生、甚至是研究所畢業生都找不到工作。舉例來說，我的表哥偉任剛從一所名聲響亮的大學畢業，卻還在找工作。我希望這次的全球金融風暴快快結束。

朗讀 CD 第 21 軌

互動光碟

15-4 解析 Language Focus

1. an avid reader 熱愛閱讀的人，an avid baseball fan 棒球迷，也可以加上動詞 take，如：

   ✎ He took an avid interest in hip hop music.
   他熱愛嘻哈音樂。

2. depress（動詞），depressed（過去分詞），depressing（現在分詞），depression（名詞）

   ✎ My low English score depresses me.
   英文分數低讓我沮喪。

   這句話也可以寫成下面兩個句型：

   ✎ I am depressed about my low English score.
   我因英文分數低而感到沮喪。

   ✎ My low English score is depressing.
   我糟糕的英文成績令人沮喪。

   depression 則指憂鬱症。

   ✎ I am not suffering from depression now.
   我現在不為憂鬱症所苦了。

   depression 也有經濟蕭條的意思，比 recession 更嚴重。

3. unemployment＝unemployment rate 失業率

   the unemployed 失業的人

   ✎ I was employed by IBM, but now I am unemployed.
   我過去受雇於 IBM，但現在失業了。

　　👂　The unemployed can receive 9 months of unemployment benefits
　　　　失業者可領九個月的失業救濟金。

4.　layoff 名詞，lay off 動詞，be laid off 被動式，laid-off 形容詞

　　👂　He was upset by his recent layoff.
　　　　最近被解雇，他很不開心。

　　👂　The company will lay off many employees.
　　　　這家公司會解雇很多員工。

　　👂　He was laid off by this company.
　　　　他被這家公司解雇了。

　　👂　The company rehired some of the laid-off employees.
　　　　這家公司重新聘用一些被解雇的員工。

5.　drop out of(from) school 是學生主動輟學，be expelled 是被學校退學，
　　dropout 中輟生

　　👂　He decided to drop out of school for a year.
　　　　他決定休學一年

　　👂　He was expelled from school because he had cheated on a test.
　　　　他因考試作弊被退學。

　　👂　He helps high school dropouts return to school.
　　　　他幫助高中中輟生重返學校。

6.　DINK（頂客族）＝double income no kids 雙薪沒小孩的人

　　用來形容名詞，位在該名詞前的兩或三個字形成的詞組，要用連字號相
　　連，如：

　　👂　double-income family 雙薪家庭

　　　　three-year-old kid 三歲小孩

　　　　brown-eyed girl 棕色眼睛的女孩

　　　　two-story house 兩層樓的房子

7. close 動詞，closure 名詞，closed 形容詞

   ◊ Close the door, please.
   請關門。

   ◊ The shop closes at 10:00 P.M.
   這家店晚上 10 點打烊。

   ◊ The typhoon has led to the closure of the roads.
   這次颱風造成道路封閉。

   ◊ The shop is closed now.
   這家店現在打烊了。

8. The government has distributed consumption coupons（which are worth NT$3600）to every Taiwanese citizen. 句中的 which are worth NT$3600 是形容 consumption coupons 的子句

   worth 是形容詞，後面接動名詞。

   ◊ It is worth trying.
   值得一試。

   ◊ This house is worth buying.
   這棟房子值得買。

9. anxious 形容詞，anxiety 名詞

   ◊ He is an anxious person.
   他是個令人焦慮的人。

   ◊ Most students have anxieties about their schoolwork.
   大部分學生擔心他們學校的課業。

10. undergraduate student 大學生，graduate student 研究生，high school graduate 高中畢業生，college graduate 大學畢業生

11. 大學畢業可以拿到學士學位 bachelor's degree。研究所畢業可以拿到碩士學位 master's degree 或博士學位 Ph.D.

12. global 全球的，globalization 全球化，local 本土的，localization 本土化，如果把兩個字結合，就成了 glocalization 全球在地化

15-5-1 選選看

1. She went out _____ the heavy rain.
   (a) despite　(b) although　(c) because

2. _____ she was late, the others were all on time.
   (a) While　(b) In spite of　(c) Because

3. They went hiking, _____ it was raining.
   (a) despite　(b) due to　(c) though

4. I couldn't sleep _____ the noise.
   (a) because　(b) because of　(c) despite

5. He accepted the job _____ the low salary.
   (a) because　(b) in spite of　(c) thanks to

6. He passed the exam _____ he didn't study hard.
   (a) though　(b) despite　(c) because

7. _____ Peter has a car, he walks to work.
   (a) Even if　(b) Even though　(c) Because

8. His parents wouldn't buy him a scooter, _____ they had money.
   (a) even if　(b) despite　(c) due to

9. _____ she likes animals, she doesn't want a rabbit.
   (a) Even though　(b) Even if　(c) Because

10. She flunked the English final exam, _____ working very hard.
    (a) because of　(b) due to　(c) despite

11. They hardly see each other, _____ they live in the same town.

  (a) despite　(b) though　(c) because

12. _____ the cold weather, everyone showed up.

  (a) Despite　(b) Even if　(c) Because

13. _____ he lost lots of money, he will continue donating money to the poor.

  (a) Even though　(b) Even　(c) Despite

14. I wouldn't do it, _____ I had time.

  (a) even if　(b) even though　(c) even

15. His success is _____ his hard work.

  (a) owing　(b) due to　(c) because

16. They decided to close the road _____ the typhoon.

  (a) thanks to　(b) even　(c) because of

17. I finished the project, _____ your advice.

  (a) because　(b) even though　(c) thanks to

18. _____ our lack of confidence, we lost the game.

  (a) Owing to　(b) Even　(c) Despite

19. I didn't go out _____ the typhoon that hit Taiwan last night.

  (a) because　(b) because of　(c) despite

20. _____ the fact that I am an avid reader, I never read science fiction(科幻小說).

  (a) In spite　(b) Despite　(c) Although

15-5-2填填看（＊注意：句子第一個字母要用大寫。）

even, even though, even if

1. That's easy. _____ a child can answer it.

2. She is going to have problems finding a job _____ she graduated from a renowned university.

3. _____ he's 35 years old now, he's still like a little kid.

4. He didn't _____ look at me at the party.

5. I can still remember the story, _____ I read this novel when I was young.

6. I love this book, _____ most of my friends hate it.

7. They wouldn't move from Taiwan, _____ there were many typhoons and earthquakes.

8. She married Peter, _____ none of her friends likes him.

9. _____ it rained yesterday, I still went cycling（騎腳踏車）.

10. _____ it rains tomorrow, I will still go cycling.

11. He can't cook. He doesn't _____ know how to use the rice cooker（電鍋）.

12. I would ride the bike to school, _____ I had a scooter.（事實：I don't have a scooter.）

13. He didn't believe me, _____ I told him the truth.

14. They wear sweaters, _____ in the hot summer.

15. He can't run very fast. _____ I can run faster than him.

15-5-3問答

1. What kind of depressing words did the writer see in the paper?

   _____

2. What did Jie Ming tell the writer after the ball game?

   _____

3. What might Jie Ming do if his parents can't find a job?

_____

4. Why are some double-income families in trouble?

_____

5. Who distributed Taiwanese citizens consumption coupons?

_____

6. What are the consumption coupons for?

_____

7. Does the writer's parents cut back on his pocket money?

_____

8. Why are many college graduates anxious?

_____

9. Has Weiren, the writer's cousin, found a job yet?

_____

10. What is the writer's hope about the global financial crisis?

_____

15-5-4 改錯

1. My mom never uses the air conditioner, even it is hot.
2. His high score was due to he worked very hard.
3. Mom was very upset even I got a good score.
4. Despite of the rain, we enjoyed our trip to Yilan.
5. I didn't go cycling because the rain.
6. This scooter is not worth to buy.
7. I see her every day, I've never spoken to her although.
8. Our anxiety was thanks to the high unemployment in Taiwan.
9. Even if I got my own consumption coupons, I gave them to Mom.
10. He isn't depressed even he was laid off.

11. Despite he dropped out of school, he continued studying.

12. Many people lost their jobs because business closures and downsizing.

13. Jie Ming would take some odd jobs even his parents had jobs.

14. Many restaurants went out of business because the recession.

15. Thanks to he gave me some good advice, I could find a job.

16. My cousin is still job hunting despite he graduated from a renowned university.

17. Although their double income, they can't afford a car.

18. Mom unplugged the electric appliances due to she wanted to save energy.

19. No one is buying this book even it is so interesting.

20. Because he has often helped me, so I should help him this time.

15-5-5英文該怎麼寫？

1. 就算他不來，我也會去看電影。

　＿＿＿＿＿＿＿＿＿＿＿＿＿＿＿＿＿＿＿＿＿＿＿＿＿

2. 即使他來了，我們也沒有去看電影。

　＿＿＿＿＿＿＿＿＿＿＿＿＿＿＿＿＿＿＿＿＿＿＿＿＿

3. 即使他工作很努力，還是被解雇了。

　＿＿＿＿＿＿＿＿＿＿＿＿＿＿＿＿＿＿＿＿＿＿＿＿＿

4. 他被解雇是因為公司沒有生意。

　＿＿＿＿＿＿＿＿＿＿＿＿＿＿＿＿＿＿＿＿＿＿＿＿＿

5. 這台冷氣雖然不貴，但我決定還是不買。（...not expensive...）

　＿＿＿＿＿＿＿＿＿＿＿＿＿＿＿＿＿＿＿＿＿＿＿＿＿

6. 因為他對時事沒興趣，所以不讀報紙。

　＿＿＿＿＿＿＿＿＿＿＿＿＿＿＿＿＿＿＿＿＿＿＿＿＿

7. 因為拿到了消費券，所以我們都去買東西（go shopping）。

　＿＿＿＿＿＿＿＿＿＿＿＿＿＿＿＿＿＿＿＿＿＿＿＿＿

8. 他什麼都不知道，甚至連全球金融危機也不知道（He doesn't know anything...）

　＿＿＿＿＿＿＿＿＿＿＿＿＿＿＿＿＿＿＿＿＿＿＿＿＿

9. 因為經濟不景氣，許多餐廳都關門大吉。(Due to...)

   _____

10. 為了刺激消費，政府發消費券給每位台灣公民。(To boost...)

   _____

11. 這部爛電影(lousy movie)不值得看。

   _____

12. 這棟兩層樓房值得買。

   _____

第十六課 Unit 16

你説、我説、他説

互動光碟

　　親愛的讀者，恭喜你過五關、斬六將，順利進入高級本下冊的最後一課。這一課我們來談談小說裡常出現的人物對話，這些對話的書寫方式，中英文不盡相同，我們現在以兩個例子來說明。台灣小說家王文興在一篇名為〈母親〉的短篇小說裡有以下的對話：

　　他問：「這麼熱的天，你媽媽在家做什麼事呢？」

　　「她在睡覺。」他壓低了聲音說。

　　和中文小說一樣，英文文章或小說裡也常出現角色間的對話，不過引用對話所用的冒號和引號與中文不太一樣，如美國著名的兒童文學家懷特(E. B. White 1899-1985)所寫的《夏綠蒂的網》(*Charlotte's Web*)第一章，當小女孩芬兒發現父親拿把斧頭正要「處理」一隻剛出生的瘦弱小豬時，與父親有段精彩的對話：

"Please don't kill it!" she sobbed. "It's unfair." Mr. Arable stopped walking. "Fern," he said gently, "You will have to learn to control yourself." "Control myself?" yelled Fern. "This is a matter of life and death, and you talk about controlling myself."

　　請看這段父女對話的中文翻譯，並請特別注意中英文引用他人說的話時，標點符號不同的地方在哪裡：

　　「求求你，別殺牠！」她啜泣著：「這實在太不公平了！」

　　艾蕊柏先生停下了腳步。

　　「芬兒，」他溫柔的說：「妳應該學學控制自己的情緒。」

　　「控制我的情緒？」芬兒叫道：「這是一件攸關生死的事情，你卻在跟我討論控制情緒！」(《夏綠蒂的網》黃可凡譯)

　　由上面例子看來，直接引用他人的話，字字句句都要出自說話者的口中，完全不能更改。用英文直接引用他人的話要怎麼寫呢？
引號該如何用呢？請看下面的說明：

I. 某人問或某人說(sb. asked 或 sb. said)，後面接逗點，而引用的
　 句子和標點符號都放在引號裡面。如：

　　🦻 He asked, "Is English very difficult to learn?"
　　　 他問：「英文是不是很難學？」

　　🦻 She said, "No, not at all."
　　　 她說：「不，一點也不難。」

　　也可以把直接引用的句子放在前面，說話的人放在後面，不過
　要注意如果引用的句尾是句點，這時候要改為逗點，如：

　　🦻 "No, not at all," she said.

II. 只有直接引用別人的話時，才用引號，如：

　　🦻 He said, "I am very thirsty and hungry."
　　　 他說：「我既渴又餓。」

　　間接轉述他人的話時不用引號，代名詞、標點符號、時態都須
　跟著改(會於 VI 仔細說明)。如：

　　🦻 He said that he was very thirsty and hungry.
　　　 他說他既渴又餓。

III. 引用的話中夾著他人說的話時，裡面的引言要放在單引號裡 '...'
　　 如：

　　🦻 She told me, "Your mom said, 'you should be home by 10:00 P.M.'"
　　　 她告訴我：「你媽媽說：『你得10點前回家。』」

IV. 引用的話可以分開來寫，如：

　　✎　"Mom was very upset," said Jie Ming, "because she noticed a pile of greasy dishes sitting in the sink."

　　　　「媽很不高興，」傑明說：「因為她注意到水槽裡堆著一堆油膩的碗盤。」

V. 如果引用的話較長，用冒號帶出引言，而不用引號框住引言。如：

　　✎　Canadian novelist Carol Shields wrote: We love fiction because it possesses the texture of the real. The characters in a novel resemble, more or less, ourselves.

　　　　加拿大小說家 Carol Shields 寫道：我們喜歡讀小說，因為小說具有真實世界的感覺。小說中的人物多多少少跟我們自己有些相像。

VI. 直接引用句（direct speech）如何改寫成間接敘述句（indirect speech）？以第三者的口氣敘述某人說了什麼時，需要改變時態、人稱和時間：

　　1. 現在式→過去式

　　✎　She said, "It's hot." → She said（that）it was hot.

　　　　她說：「天氣很熱。」→ 她說天氣很熱。

　　2. 現在進行式→過去進行式

　　✎　He said, "I'm reading online news." → He said（that）he was reading online news.

　　　　他說：「我正在看網路新聞。」→ 他說他正在看網路新聞。

　　3. 現在完成式→過去完成式

🔈 She said, "I've lived here since 2001." → She said (that) she had lived here since 2001.

她說：「我從 2001 年起住在這裡。」→她說她從 2001 年起住在這裡。

4. 過去式→過去完成式

🔈 He said, "I went camping yesterday." → He said (that) he had gone camping yesterday.

他說：「我昨天去露營。」→ 他說他昨天去露營。

5. 未來式→過去未來式

🔈 She said, "I will go to Kaohsiung tomorrow." → She said (that) she would go to Kaohsiung tomorrow.

她說：「我明天會去高雄。」→ 她說她明天會去高雄。

6. 如果引言是不變的事實，時態可以改，也可以不改。如：

👂 He told me, "My name is Paul." → He told me (that) his name was (is) Paul.

他告訴我：「我的名字是保羅。」→ 他告訴我他的名字是保羅。

除了常用的 said、told、asked 外，還可以用以下動詞(皆以過去式呈現)接引用的句子，如：

inquired(詢問)，admitted(承認)，wrote(寫)，added(補充)，continued(繼續說)，debated(爭論)，argued(反駁)，claimed(聲稱)，cried out(大叫)，shouted(大叫)，yelled(大叫)，declared(宣布)，whispered(輕聲說)，ordered(命令)，interrupted(插嘴)，demanded(要求)，proclaimed(聲明)，answered(回答)，murmured(喃喃自語)等等。

VII. 直接問句改成間接問句就是把問句改成敘述句：

He asked, "Will you come?"

他問：「你會來嗎？」

→He asked if I would come.（或 He asked whether I would come or not.）

他問我是否會來。

→He would like to know if I would come.

→He was wondering if I would come.

他想知道我會不會來。

She asked, "When does the restaurant close?"

她問：「這家餐廳什麼時候打烊？」

→She asked when the restaurant closed.

她問這家餐廳什麼時候打烊。

He asked her, "How much are these jeans?"

他問她：「這條牛仔褲要多少錢？」

＊注意：牛仔褲是複數。

→He asked her how much these jeans are.

他問她這條牛仔褲要多少錢。

She asked, "Why do I have to sign my name here?"

她問：「我為什麼得在這裡簽名？」

→She asked why she had to sign her name here.

她問為何她要在這裡簽名。

III. 直接命令句改為間接命令句：

She ordered him, "Make your bed and tidy up your desk."

她命令他：「鋪床並整理書桌。」

→She ordered him <u>to</u> make his bed and tidy up his desk.

她命令他去鋪床並整理書桌。

He shouted, "Be quiet!"

他大叫：「安靜！」

→He shouted to (at) everyone to be quiet.

他叫每個人安靜下來。

＊注意：shouted to 大聲地叫；shout at 生氣地喊

朗讀 CD 第 22 軌

互動光碟

16-1 生字 Vocabulary

receive	(v.)收到（receive, received, received）
low-paying	(adj.)低薪的
in hand	(ph.)在手
check out	(ph.)親自去看看
book fair	(ph.)書展
main entrance	(ph.)主要入口處
guest of honor	(ph.)主題國
admit	(v.)承認（admit, admitted, admitted）
apart from	(ph.)除了
spicy	(adj.)重口味的
scenery	(n.)風景
spot	(v.)注意到（spot, spotted, spotted）
entitled	(v.)給……取名（entitle, entitled, entitled）
judgment	(n.)判決、審判
novelist	(n.)小說家

n.＝名詞　ph.＝詞組　v.＝動詞　adv.＝副詞　adj.＝形容詞

somber-looking	(adj.)貌似深沉的
autograph	(n.)簽名
book signing	(ph.)簽書會
satisfied	(adj.)滿足的
realize	(v.)知道、瞭解到、發現(realize, realized, realized)
for the sake of	(ph.)為了
severe	(adj.)嚴峻的

朗讀 CD 第 23 軌

互動光碟

16-2 課文 Text

This morning I **received** a text message from Jie Ming. He told me that both of his parents had luckily found full-time, though **low-paying**, jobs[1]. Now with consumption coupons **in hand**[2], he wanted to **check out** the Taipei **Book Fair**[3] and buy some books. I felt a bit bored from staying home all day, so I asked him to meet me at the **main entrance** to the book fair.

This year's **guest of honor**[4] is Thailand. I have to **admit** that, **apart from** the country's **spicy** food and beautiful **scenery**, I hardly know anything about Thailand. At the book fair, I **spotted** a novel **entitled**[5] *The Judgment*[6], which was written by a Thai[7] **novelist**. There was a long line of people waiting to get the **somber-looking**, long-haired[8] writer's **autograph**.

I asked Jie Ming, "Do you want to get his autograph?" He didn't say yes or no, but answered jokingly, "We used to line up for pop singers' autographs, and now here we are at a **book signing**!"

Carrying *The Judgment* along with the other books we'd bought, Jie Ming and I went home **satisfied**[9]. I know that when Mom sees the books I bought, she will **realize** that I don't just read **for the sake of** passing exams. This winter may be especially cold due to the **severe** financial crisis; however, with the books I bought, I feel rich!

16-3 課文翻譯

今天早上我收到傑明的簡訊。他告訴我他的父母幸運地找到了薪水雖然不高卻是全職的工作。現在他手裡有消費券，想去台北書展看看並買些書。我覺得整天在家有點無聊，所以要他在書展正門口等我。

今年的主題國是泰國，除了泰國的辛辣食物和美麗風景外，我得承認自己對泰國所知不多。在書展展場我注意到一本泰國小說家所寫、名為《判決》的小說。大排長龍的人潮等著拿到這位外表深沉的長髮作家的親筆簽名。

我問傑明：「你要不要他的簽名？」傑明不置可否，卻開玩笑地回答說：「我們從前都排隊要流行歌手的簽名，而現在卻在這裡參加簽書會！」

我們抱著《判決》和我們買的其他書回家，覺得心滿意足。我知道媽媽看到我買的書一定會瞭解我不只是為通過考試而讀書。今年冬天因嚴峻的金融風暴來襲而顯得特別冷颼颼，但有了我買的這些書，我覺得自己很「富足」！

朗讀 CD 第 24 軌

 互動光碟

16-4 解析 Language Focus

1. He told me that both of his parents had luckily found full-time, though low-paying, jobs. 這句另一個寫法是：He told me that both of his parents had luckily found full-time jobs, though low-paying. 他的父母找到工作這件事發生在他告訴我這件事之前，故用過去完成式

2. 有幾個關於「手 hand」的片語，很容易混淆：

   give sb. a hand 幫助某人，助某人一臂之力

   ◎ She often gives me a hand when I need help.
   　她通常在我需要幫助時助我一臂之力。

   give sb. a free hand to V 放手讓某人做某事

   ◎ My parents gave me a free hand to choose my major.
   　我的父母讓我自由選擇我要讀的系。

   hand-me-downs 家中傳下來的舊衣服

   ◎ I often wore my brother's hand-me-downs when I was young.
   　我小時候常穿哥哥的舊衣服。

   on hand 在手邊，很容易取得

   ◎ I didn't have any tools on hand to fix the broken chair.
   　我手邊沒有任何工具來修這張壞掉的椅子。

   by hand 用手做

   ◎ She made this table by hand.
   　她親自動手做了這張桌子。

hand in hand 牽手

🦻　They are walking hand in hand.
　　他們手牽手走著。

at hand 快到了

🦻　The end of the world is at hand.
　　世界末日即將到來。

in hand 擁有

🦻　He has 100 euros in hand.
　　他手中有 100 歐元。

3.　台北國際書展在每年 1 月 27 日至 2 月 1 日舉行

4.　guest of honor 每個國際書展都有一個「主題國」，2008 年台北國際書展的主
　　題國是泰國，書展現場介紹該國豐富的文化產業

5.　The novel（which was）entitled *The Judgment* was written by a Thai novelist.
　　英文書名用斜體字或加底線，如：*The Judgment* 或 The Judgment

6.　judge 判決（動詞），judge 法官（名詞），judgment 判決（名詞），judgmental 批
　　判性的；動輒評頭論足的、動輒指責人的（形容詞）

7.　Thailand 泰國，Thai 泰國人，Thai 泰國的（如：Thai food 泰國菜）

8.　long-haired 是由兩個形容詞所組成的形容詞，其他例子如下：

　　🦻　a dark-haired girl 黑髮女孩
　　　　a middle-aged woman 中年婦人
　　　　a near-sighted student 近視的學生
　　　　a blue-color shirt 藍襯衫

9.　形容詞 satisfied 和 satisfying 很容易混淆，基本上附 ed 的形容詞通常表達一
　　個人自己的感覺，如：我很滿意他的工作。I was satisfied with his work. 附
　　ing 的形容詞則是描述一個人或一件事的狀態，如：他做的工作令人滿意：His
　　work was satisfying.

這類的形容詞很多，例如：

☝ bored → She is bored with her job.
她覺得她的工作很無聊。

☝ boring → Her job is boring.
她的工作很無聊。

☝ interested → She is interested in this novel.
她對這本小說很感興趣（她想讀這本小說）。

☝ interesting → This novel is interesting.
這本小說很有意思。

☝ disgusted → I was disgusted by the dead cockroach.
我覺得這隻死蟑螂真噁心。

☝ disgusting → This dead cockroach is disgusting.
這隻死蟑螂真令人作嘔。

☝ disappointed → I was disappointed in this movie.
我對這部電影很失望。

☝ disappointing→This movie was disappointing.
這部電影令人失望。

其他這類形容詞還很多，讀者可舉一反三，如：

👂 annoyed 覺得惱火　　　annoying 惱人的

　　amused 覺得好玩　　　amusing 好玩的

　　confused 覺得困惑　　　confusing 困惑的

　　embarrassed 覺得很糗　　embarrassing 很糗的

　　excited 覺得刺激　　　exciting 很興奮的

　　exhausted 覺得很累　　　exhausting 累死人的

　　surprised 感覺吃驚　　　surprising 吃驚的

16-5 練習題

16-5-1 選選看

1. Apart from _____, I don't like any other sports.
   (a)swim　(b)swam　(c)swimming

2. She told me that she _____ a novel worth reading.
   (a)find　(b)have found　(c)had found

3. "I don't know the names of any Thai pop singers," he _____.
   (a)had admitted　(b)admited　(c)admitted

4. I couldn't sleep because of the _____ noise.
   (a)annoy　(b)annoying　(c)annoyed

5. She gets _____ easily.（她很容易感到尷尬。）
   (a)embarrass　(b)embarrassing　(c)embarrassed

6. Peter always talks about himself. He is indeed a _____ person.
   (a)bore　(b)boring　(c)bored

7. He wasn't sure whether she _____ his text message or not.
   (a)receives　(b)has received　(c)had received

8. I was wondering if she _____ this novel before.
   (a)reads　(b)have read　(c)had read

9. It has rained a lot. This winter has been really _____.
   (a)depress　(b)depressed　(c)depressing

10. Working at the convenience store was quite an _____ experience for her.
    (a)excitement　(b)excited　(c)exciting

11. I asked her if she wanted to swim with us, but she wasn't _____.
    (a) interests   (b) interested   (c) interesting

12. I didn't know where the book signing was. I was very _____.
    (a) confuse   (b) confused   (c) confusing

13. Do you know _____?
    (a) who is the novelist   (b) who the novelist is   (c) who was the novelist

14. Could you tell me _____.
    (a) where I can buy this comic book?

    (b) where can I buy this comic book?

    (c) where do I buy this comic book?

15. My trip to Thailand was _____.
    (a) shocked   (b) confused   (c) exhausting

16. It was _____ that he had dropped out of school.
    (a) surprise   (b) surprised   (c) surprising

17. I don't know why he always looks so _____.
    (a) bore   (b) bored   (c) boring

18. My mom wasn't satisfied _____ the work I did.
    (a) in   (b) by   (c) with

19. We were all very surprised that he _____ the exam.
    (a) passes   (b) passed   (c) passing

20. He asked me which book is the most _____.
    (a) interest   (b) interested   (c) interesting

16-5-2 填填看(請選最適合的字填入空格中。)

interesting, interested, bored, confusing, confused, exciting, excited, tiring, tired, annoying, annoyed, amused, depressing, depressed, satisfied, disappointing, disappointed, shocking, shocked

1. Most teenagers(青少年)are not _____ in reading newspapers.
2. They were _____ when they first heard the terrible news. Some had their mouths wide opened; others started crying.
3. I couldn't believe that they had spent so much money making this lousy film. It was so _____.
4. She is very _____ because she's starting a new job next Monday.
5. Even if she got high scores and passed the exam, her parents wouldn't be _____.
6. She became _____ after her dog's sudden death.
7. I could feel that he was _____ by their loud music even though he didn't say a word.
8. Most students didn't understand what the teacher was saying. They looked _____.
9. If the lesson is _____, students won't get bored.
10. Kids were _____ by the tricks that the monkey did. They all laughed and clapped their hands.

16-5-3問答

1. Who sent a text message to the writer this morning?

    _____

2. Did Jie Ming's parents get full-time or part-time jobs?

    _____

3. How would Jie Ming like to spend his consumption coupons?

    _____

4. Where did the writer ask Jie Ming to meet him?

   _____

5. What does the writer know about Thailand?

   _____

6. Who wrote *The Judgment*?

   _____

7. What did many people in the book fair line up for?

   _____

8. Whose autographs did Jie Ming and the writer used to get?

   _____

9. Did the writer buy the Thai novel, *The Judgment*?

   _____

10. Does the writer read books only for the sake of passing exams?

    _____

16-5-4 改錯

1. He asked her meet him at the main entrance to the building.
2. I was wondering what kind of books did they buy.
3. His mom asked him when will he go to the book fair
4. She told me that she watching a great movie the other day.
5. "I just thought of something," he announce, "Tomorrow is my birthday."
6. He whispered to me, "This scooter was not worth buying."
7. I forgot where did I buy this novel.
8. He asked her who is your favorite novelist.
9. He said that she takes a shower now.
10. He wanted to know I could go to the book fair with him or not.
11. I finally realized that *The Judgment* was written by a Thailand novelist.
12. He argued that many people lost their jobs because business downsizing.

13. He told me happily that he get the novelist's autograph.

14. I was embarrassing because I forgot today was her birthday.

15. The novelist looked exhausting after signing so many books and talking to so many people.

16. We were all surprising when they got married.

17. Her exam score seemed disappointed.

18. She feels boring from doing the same thing every day.

19. Mom told me, "If I was you, I wouldn't just bury my nose in textbooks."

20. They were shocking to hear about the earthquake.

16-5-5英文該怎麼寫？

1. 如果我沒有去書展，我就不會遇到那位泰國小說家。(If I hadn't gone to...)

_____

2. 就算他們去了書展，也不會參加簽書會。(Even if they had gone to...)

_____

3. 他媽媽說：「我現在才知道你讀書不只是為了通過考試。」

_____

4. 他問我是否知道哪一個國家是主題國。(He asked me if I...)

_____

5. 很多人排隊為了要這位小說家的簽名。

_____

6. 媽媽叫我把電器用品(electric appliances)的插頭拔起來。(Mom asked me...)

_____

7. 媽媽很興奮拿到了駕照。(Mom was... when she...)

_____

8. 今年的書展真令人滿意。

   _____

9. 我叫他去找圖書館有沒有今天的報紙。(I asked him to find out...)

   _____

10. 她告訴我她今天看的電影很令人失望。(She told me that...)

    _____

朗讀 CD 第 25 軌

互動光碟

附錄

不規則動詞三態變化表

I. 三態同形（動詞原形、過去式、過去分詞完全相同）

動詞原形	過去式	過去分詞	現在分詞
burst 爆裂、突然……	burst	burst	bursting
cost 值、花（多少錢）	cost	cost	costing
cut 切、剪、割	cut	cut	cutting
hit 打擊、到達	hit	hit	hitting
hurt 受傷	hurt	hurt	hurting
let 讓	let	let	letting
put 放	put	put	putting
quit 停止	quit	quit	quitting
read 讀	read	read	reading
set 安置	set	set	setting
shut 關	shut	shut	shutting
spread 展開	spread	spread	spreading

*注意：read的過去式和過去分詞拼法與動詞原形一樣，但發音不同。

II. 一、三態相同（動詞原形、過去分詞相同）

動詞原形	過去式	過去分詞	現在分詞
become 成為	became	become	becoming
come 來	came	come	coming
overcome 克服	overcame	overcome	overcoming
run 跑	ran	run	running

III. 二、三態相同（過去式、過去分詞相同）

動詞原形	過去式	過去分詞	現在分詞
bring 帶來	brought	brought	bringing
build 建造	built	built	building
buy 買	bought	bought	buying
catch 接住、捉到	caught	caught	catching
deal 處理	dealt	dealt	dealing
dig 挖	dug	dug	digging
feed 餵	fed	fed	feeding
feel 覺得	felt	felt	feeling
fight 爭吵	fought	fought	fighting
find 找到	found	found	finding
hang 掛	hung	hung	hanging
have(has) 有	had	had	having
hear 聽	heard	heard	hearing
hold 握住	held	held	holding
keep 保持	kept	kept	keeping
lay 置放	laid	laid	laying
lead 引導、領導	led	led	leading
leave 離開	left	left	leaving

lose 遺失	lost	lost	losing
make 使、做	made	made	making
mean 意指	meant	meant	meaning
meet 遇到	met	met	meeting
pay 付錢	paid	paid	paying
say 說	said	said	saying
seek 尋找	sought	sought	seeking
sell 賣	sold	sold	selling
send 寄、送	sent	sent	sending
shine 發光	shone	shone	shining
sit 坐	sat	sat	sitting
sleep 睡	slept	slept	sleeping
spend 花(時間、金錢)	spent	spent	spending
stand 站	stood	stood	standing
teach 教	taught	taught	teaching
tell 告訴	told	told	telling
think 想	thought	thought	thinking
understand 了解	understood	understood	understanding
win 贏	won	won	winning

IV. 一、二、三態各不相同(動詞原形、過去式、過去分詞各不相同)

動詞原形	過去式	過去分詞	現在分詞
be 是	was/were	been	being
begin 開始	began	begun	beginning
blow 吹	blew	blown	blowing

break 打破	broke	broken	breaking
choose 選擇	chose	chosen	choosing
do（does）做	did	done	doing
drink 喝	drank	drunk	drinking
drive 開車	drove	driven	driving
eat 吃	ate	eaten	eating
fall 落下	fell	fallen	falling
fly 飛	flew	flown	flying
forbid 禁止	forbade	forbidden	forbidding
forget 忘記	forgot	forgotten	forgetting
forgive 原諒	forgave	forgiven	forgiving
freeze 結冰、使凍住	froze	frozen	freezing
get 拿	got	gotten	getting
give 給與	gave	given	giving
go 走	went	gone	going
grow 生長	grew	grown	growing
hide 藏	hid	hidden	hiding
know 知道	knew	known	knowing
lie 躺	lay	lain	lying
mistake 弄錯、誤解、把……誤認為	mistook	mistaken	mistaking
ride 騎	rode	ridden	riding
ring 響	rang	rung	ringing
rise 升起、起床	rose	risen	rising
see 看	saw	seen	seeing

shake 搖動	shook	shaken	shaking
sing 唱	sang	sung	singing
speak 說	spoke	spoken	speaking
steal 偷	stole	stolen	stealing
swim 游泳	swam	swum	swimming
take 拿去	took	taken	taking
tear 撕開、撕裂	tore	torn	tearing
throw 丟、擲	threw	thrown	throwing
wake 醒來	woke	waken	waking
wear 穿	wore	worn	wearing
write 寫	wrote	written	writing

總複習

I. 選擇題

1. We are waiting for the bus _____ the bus stop.
    (a) at　(b) on　(c) in

2. His office is _____ the tenth floor of the building.
    (a) at　(b) on　(c) in

3. Many interesting activities will be held _____ campus this semester(學期).
    (a) at　(b) on　(c) in

4. He didn't make his bed, nor _____ he do the dishes.
    (a) is　(b) does　(c) did

5. I can't speak French, nor _____ I speak German(德文).
    (a) did　(b) can　(c) X

6. _____ you hand in homework on time, I won't flunk you in English.
    (a) Although　(b) Even　(c) As long as

7. _____ attract foreign students, the school offers many scholarships.
    (a) Despite　(b) In order to　(c) After

8. _____ all the courses I am taking, I like math the most.
    (a) Between　(b) Among　(c) After

9. _____ this summer, I have been writing my blog.
    (a) Before　(b) When　(c) Since

10. I like _____ coffee my cousin made.
    (a) X　(b) the　(c) a

11. What do you usually eat for _____ breakfast?
    (a) the　(b) a　(c) X

12. She plays _____ badminton twice a week.
    (a) the (b) a (c) X

13. My sister-in-law taught me how to play _____ guitar.
    (a) the (b) a (c) an

14. They will take a trip to _____ USA this summer.
    (a) the (b) a (c) X

15. She failed the entrance exam, _____ surprised everyone.
    (a) what (b) which (c) at which

16. She is the girl _____ I go out.
    (a) who (b) whom (c) with whom

17. Do you know the people _____ across from us?
    (a) live (b) lived (c) living

18. The cat _____ the leftovers(剩菜) is a stray cat(野貓).
    (a) eat (b) ate (c) eating

19. The book _____ as the best novel of 2009 was written by my uncle.
    (a) choosing (b) chosen (c) choice

20. If it _____ tomorrow, I will not go cycling with you.
    (a) rains (b) will rain (c) raining

21. I wish I _____ speak a European language(歐洲語言).
    (a) can (b) could (c) do

22. If I had listened to what she said, I _____ my camera.
    (a) wouldn't lose (b) wouldn't lost (c) wouldn't have lost

23. We have to save electricity around our house _____ the recent energy crisis.
    (a) because (b) despite (c) due to

24. Mom got her driver's license _____ the rigorous written and driving tests.
    (a) after (b) although (c) due to

25. Jie Ming suggested we _____ to the coffee shop at the corner of the street.
    (a) went (b) going (c) go

26. She stared at me and said sternly, "If I _____ you, I wouldn't go."

　　(a) am　(b) was　(c) were

27. She shouted to her students _____ run.

　　(a) don't　(c) not　(c) not to

28. _____ some double-income families are in trouble because of business closures and downsizing.

　　(a) Even though　(b) Although　(c) Even

29. I asked Jie Ming _____ to get the novelist's autograph.

　　(a) would you like　(b) did you like to　(c) if he would like

30. I am very _____ about my final grades.

　　(a) anxious　(b) anxiety　(c) anxiously

II. 填充題

1. Swine flu(H1N1豬流感) and bird flu(禽流感) have _____ (spread) to humans.

2. She _____ (catch) a cold(感冒) last week.

3. Have you _____ (spot) something unusual in this room?

4. If I hadn't _____ (take) a picture of the kitten and posted it on the Internet, it would still be with us.

5. Mom and Dad were _____ (debate) whether we could keep two cats or not.

6. After the ball game, all of our friends _____ (leave) for home.

7. If her son didn't come home by 11:00PM, she would be waiting for him _____ (anxious) at the door.

8. They _____ (draw) lots to decide who would do the dishes yesterday.

9. Among the fans of the singer, I _____ (surprise) spotted my girlfriend, who was lining up to get his autograph.

10. The shopkeeper has _____ (show) me a beautiful purple lady's bike.

11. He _____ (give) my dad a 20% discount because he bought two bikes at the same time.

12. The _____ (fold) bike I bought yesterday is very light(很輕).

13. She _____ (lay) the shopping bag carefully down on the floor.

14. _____ (challenge) by her husband, she retorted, "You're not better than me."

15. Before _____ (lie) in bed, he drank a glass of milk.

16. The bus will be leaving _____ a few minutes.

17. She even works _____ Sunday mornings.

18. Mom always makes us ride bikes or _____ public transportation.

19. On the first day of our English _____ (write) class, the teacher asked us to take a test.

20. The bathroom wall started _____ (peel).

21. She has _____ (bury) the secret in her mind for 20 years.

22. Only a few households in our apartment building subscribe _____ newspapers and magazines.

23. To my surprise, I discovered that the highest _____ (pay) job in this country is translating(翻譯).

24. We were satisfied _____ the work they'd done for us.

25. He _____ (admit), "I did something that I shouldn't do."

26. He was very upset after being _____ (lay) off.

27. He _____ (drop) out of school in June and went to work at a convenience store.

28. His previous job was selling _____ (electricity) appliances.

29. During the summer in Taiwan the _____ often goes up to 38 degrees Centigrade.

30. In order to save energy, Mom has changed all of our light bulbs for energy- _____ (save) ones.

III. 改錯(有些句子有兩個錯誤)

1. They got married on last Friday.

2. Unlike his wife, he doesn't have a night life. He doesn't like going out at the night.

3. I will pick you up(接機) in the airport in Sunday morning.(有兩個錯誤)

4. The civil servant whom you met him in the office is very friendly.

5. The woman lives next door to us is a doctor.

6. Do you know the girl that Jack is dancing?

7. The museum(博物館) we wanted to visit it was closed.

8. Even he can't drive, he bought a car.

9. She doesn't enjoy the job despite it is high-paying.

10. Although she has a important job, she isn't well paying.(有兩個錯誤)

11. I like search for informations on the Internet.(有兩個錯誤).

12. This mountain bike was not belong to me.

13. I afraid of cockroaches(蟑螂).

14. She teaching me how to play the saxophone.

15. Not until he had had toothache for a week, he went to see a dentist.(有兩個錯誤)

16. The final exam, which was hold on July 1st, was very challenged. (有兩個錯誤)

17. If I didn't play computer games, I could have finished my homework on time.

18. I wish I can play tennis.

19. His mom told him don't stay up late(開夜車)playing computer games.

20. I asked her do you have to go now?

IV. 翻譯

1. 大學畢業後，我想進(get into)研究所。(After graduating from...)

_____

2. 我們訂了兩份報紙和三份雜誌。

_____

3. 我很羨慕他有份高薪的工作。(I envy him for...)

_____

4. 我買了一打(a dozen)省電燈泡。

_____

5. 他在這家電器行已工作了三年。(He has worked for...)

_____

6. 為了節省能源，他把冷氣插頭拔掉。(In order to...)

_____

7. 我三天內一定回你一封簡訊。(...within three days)

_____

8. 即使我頭痛，我也會去書展。(Even if...)

_____

9. 媽媽告訴我不要為了(for the sake of)通過考試而讀書。

_____

10. 這隻流浪貓沒有在樹上，也沒有在牆後面。(The stray cat isn't in...)

_____

11. 這位穿著條紋(striped)洋裝的女士是我的泰文老師。(The woman...)

_____

12. 我很興奮因為他送了我一台小摺當我的生日禮物(as a birthday present)。

_____

13. 他對他的英文成績(English score)很失望。

_____

14. 請告訴我美術館在哪裡。(Please tell me...)

_____

15. 爸爸建議我賣掉機車。(Dad suggested...)

_____

16. 夏天我最喜歡的水果是芒果和荔枝。

_____

17. *The Judgment*是一本你會有興趣的書。

_____

18. 我認識一個女孩她的姊姊是你的嫂嫂。(I know a girl...)

_____

19. 如果我當時讀了那本課本，英文考試就應該會過。

_____

20. 如果今天早上我吃了早餐的話，在課堂上(in class)就不會那麼餓。

_____

答案請見 pp. 205-207

習題解答

第九課　介系詞

9-5-1 選選看

1. b　2. c　3. a　4. b　5. a
6. c　7. c　8. a　9. c
10. b（at the weekend 是英式說法）
11. a　12. b　13. c　14. b　15. b
16. c　17. a　18. c　19. b　20. a
21. a　22. c　23. c　24. c.　25. b

9-5-2 選出適當的介系詞填入句子中

1. From
2. in
3. In
4. for
5. since
6. at
7. X
8. on
9. on
10. in
11. on, in
12, in
13. at
14. in
15. in
16. on, for
17. on
18. from
19. At/on
20. on
21. with
22. of
23. of
24. with
25, with
26. of
27. of
28. of
29. about
30. in
31. out of
32. on
33. in
34. by
35. on
36. on（或 at）
37. on
38. in

39. In
40. in

9-5-3 問答

1. All of their friends except for Jie Ming, Hong Sheng, and the writer.
2. He suggested they go to the coffee shop on/around corner of the street.
3. He thought they should have shaved ice at a roadside stand instead.
4. Because they were sweaty and smelly.
5. Jie Ming likes to be in charge of things.
6. He often feels lonely and pressured.
7. Hong Sheng is not used to giving opinions
8. Because Inky disappeared.
9. No, he wasn't on the balcony.
10. Inky disappeared at 10 o'clock in the morning(on July 31st).

9-5-4 改錯

1. Who will be in charge of this meeting?
2. Inky disappeared yesterday.
3. She suggested we drink some coffee first.
4. In summer we usually go to the beach.
5. There is a drug store a few steps from the school.
6. Who told you that we are jealous of you?
7. She grew lots of plants on the balcony.
8. I will show up in front of your house in ten minutes.
9. My summer vacation lasts for two months（或lasts two months）.
10. I am afraid of cockroaches.
11. On my way to school, I stopped at a roadside stand.
12. He is not used to eating at roadside stands.（或 He used to eat at roadside stands）

9-5-5 英文該怎麼寫？

1. This computer game is already out of date.
2. We're satisfied with tonight's basketball game.
3. Mom suggested I do my homework first.
4. I'm the oldest child in the family, but he's the youngest.

5. The books on my desk disappeared.
6. He didn't eat, nor did he drink.
7. In my opinion, Inky must be hiding on the balcony.
8. I am not used to going to bed before midnight.
9. They only envy you, but they are not jealous of you.
10. He searched everywhere for the lost key, but in vain. （或 He looked for his lost key everywhere, but in vain）

第十課 連接詞

10-5-1 選選看

1. b   2. c   3. b   4. c   5. b
6. b   7. a   8. b   9. b   10. c
11. b   12. c   13. a   14. c   15. b
16. b   17. c   18. b   19. a   20. c

10-5-2 選出適當的連接詞填入句子中

1. Even though
2. whenever（或 as long as, after, once）
3. Because of
4. Once（或 Whenever, After）
5. while（或 whereas）
6. wherever（或 after, once, even though, whenever）
7. After
8. Unless
9. In order to
10. Whenever（或 After, Once, As long as）
11. whereas（或 even though, while）
12. either

10-5-3 問答

1. Last night he dreamed（或 dreamt）of his cat.
2. A pink Hello Kitty was with Inky.
3. The sound of a cat woke him up.
4. He saw Inky standing right in front of him with a kitten.
5. His dad was furious.
6. His mom seemed to be debating whether they could keep two cats or not.
7. He jumped out of his bed to take out his digital camera and took some pictures of the kitten.
8. He posted them on the Internet.
9. The writer received messages from local and abroad.

10. The applicants were a single mother and a 30-year-old man.
11. He decided to interview the applicauts first.

10-5-4 改錯
1. Although I want to keep the kitten, my parents won't allow me to do so.
2. Inky came back, and so <u>did</u> the kitten.
3. I don't want to adopt a cat, and <u>neither</u> does he.
4. Because my parents didn't want to keep the kitten, I tried to find a person to adopt her. (或 My parents didn't want to keep the kitten, so I tried to find a person to adopt her.)
5. A: I don't like cats. B: Me <u>neither</u>. 或 My parents didn
6. I would like a cup of tea, and so <u>would</u> my husband.
7. I was sick, <u>but</u> I went to school.
8. Even though it is very cold, I <u>am</u> not wearing a coat.
9. Because he was tired, he went to bed early.
10. We live in an apartment, and so <u>does</u> he.

11. I can't ride a motorcycle, nor <u>can</u> I drive a car.
12. He can't play the piano, and his brother can't, <u>either</u>.

10-5-5 英文該怎麼寫？
1. Hello Kitty is a famous Japanese comic icon. (或 Hello Kitty is a famous Japanese comic character.)
2. She not only likes to play basketball, but she also likes to play badminton.
3. I received messages from Iran, Brazil, and South Africa. (或 She likes to play not only basketball but also badminton.)
4. Dad firmly told me, "We can't keep any cats!"
5. She is debating whether or not to go to see him at the bus station.
6. I like to watch science fiction movies and so does my boyfriend.
7. I can't ride a bicycle and neither can my sister.
8. I decided to walk to school, and so did my friends. (I decided to go to school on foot and so did

my friends.）

9. As long as he is willing to adopt my cat, I will immediately bring it to him. （或 As long as he is willing to adopt my cat, I will bring it to him right away.）

10. I posted all of the photos of my cats on the website. （或 I posted all of my cats photos on the website.）

第十一課　冠詞

11-5-1 選選看

1. b　2. c　　3. a　　4. b　　5. c
6. b　7. b　　8. b　　9. c　　10. b
11. c　12. c　13. a　14. a　15. a
16. a　17. c　18. b　19. b　20. c
21. c　22. b　23. b　24. a　25. a
26. c　27. c　28. c　29. b　30. c

11-5-2 填填看（＊注意：句子第一個字母要用大寫。）

1. a
2. an
3. an
4. X
5. The/An, an
6. an
7. an
8. the

9. a, X
10. a, the
11. A
12. the, X
13. X
14. the
15. The
16. The
17. An
18. X
19. an/the, the
20. an/the

11-5-3 問答

1. They said that they were animal lovers and wanted to have the cat.
2. He asked his net friends to draw lots.
3. The single mom got the cat.
4. He felt a big relief（或He felt relieved）.
5. He saw a group of people in front of a bike shop.
6. He showed the customers mountain bikes, foldable bikes, and bicycles-built-for-two.
7. He spotted his parents among them.
8. She bought a beautiful purple

lady's bike.

9. He wanted the shopkeeper to cut the price of the bikes because he was going to buy two of them at the same time.

10. He got a 20% discount.

11. He suggested he get rid of his scooter because gas prices had hit an all-time high.

12. His dad suggested he buy a used bike. (或 His dad suggested he buy a second-hand bike.)

11-5-4 改錯

1. Is there a post office near here? I need to go to the post office.

2. My professor is a European.

3. Furniture is getting more and more expensive.

4. Please give me some advice. (或 Please give me a piece of advice.)

5. I love the '70 music.

6. He lives in an old house.

7. He is my friend. (或 He is a friend of mine.)

8. I need information about that singer's birthday.

9. I am tired. I need to go to bed now.

10. It has been an extremely hot summer vacation.

11. What did you do with the ice cream I bought?

12. I would like you to meet Dr. Wong.

13. I was surprised to find out that he can speak the Thai language.

14. I took a trip to the USA last summer.

15. In a day or two, I will tell you some/a piece of good news.

11-5-5 英文該怎麼寫？

1. This is the happiest day of my life.

2. We went bowling last night.

3. Last week, my boyfriend and I toured Kenting on a bicycle-built-for-two.

4. Having finished taking the High School Entrance Exam, I felt a relief/I felted relieved. (或 I felt relieved after I finished taking the High School Entrance Exam. 或 After finishing taking the High school Entrance

Exam, I felt relieved.)

5. I got a 5% discount when I bought this foldable bicycle.

6. He excitedly showed me his brand new scooter.

7. The cost of living hits an all-time high.

8. I spotted the Filipino among all the students right away.

9. All of the unemployed have found work/jobs.

10. He suggested that I first find a job.

第十二課　子句

12-5-1 選選看

1. a　2. a　3. c　4. b　5. b
6. a　7. a　8. a　9. c　10. b
11. b　12. c　13. b　14. c　15. a
16. b　17. b　18. a　19. c　20. a
21. b　22. a　23. b　24. c　25. c

12-5-2 填填看

1. where/how
2. whether
3. what
4. which
5. who
6. with which
7. that

8. with whom
9. whose
10. in which/where
11. when
12. why
13. how/when/why
14. which
15. whose

12-5-3 問答

1. The writer's summer vacation started on July 1st.

2. His summer vacation will end on September 11th.

3. It is hot and humid.

4. He studies at a cram school.
   (或 He takes Englich and math lessons at the cram school.)

5. She banned them from using the air conditioner to save electricity.

6. They use energy-saving light bulbs.

7. She unplugged the electrical appliances to save electricity.
   (或 She unplugged the electrical appliances to reduce the electricity bills.)

8. She reminds him to shut/turn off the light.

9.　He carried a shopping bag.

10. Plastic bags are not allowed to be used in his house.

11. He is going to buy some lychees and mangoes.

12. He gave her the nickname "recycling-crazy mom."

12-5-4 改錯

1.　I don't like the boy with whom you danced.

2.　Please tell me what you did last night.

3.　Peter is the person who was talking to me in the library.

4.　This is the town where I was born. (或 This is the town in which I was born.)

5.　I found the bike that you are looking for.

6.　The house in which we live is very comfortable. (或 The house where we live is very comfortable. 或 The house which we live in is very comfortable)

7.　I will never forget the day on which (或 when) I met you.

8.　I enjoyed the trip that I took last week.

9.　Amy was the last person who/ that arrived today.

10. The trip that I took last week was quite interesting.

11. I am not sure where he lives.

12. The woman about whom you were talking is right over there.

13. This is Henry, whom you met last night.

14. *The Taipei Times*, the newspaper that you buy every day, will hire new reporters.

15. Please tell me where the ladies' room is.

16. I don't know when he is going to leave.

17. You need to find out who he is first.

18. The person who(m) we met at Tina's party called me today.

19. The book which you lent to me is very interesting.

20. The building in which my dad works is on Sanmin Road.

12-5-5 請將兩句合爲一句(用關係子句):

2.　I found the textbook that you are looking for. (或 I found the textbook which you are looking for.)

3. He wrote a novel that is named Accidental Encounter. (或 He wrote a novel of which nome is Accidental Encounter.)

4. I am carrying a shopping bag that was made by my mom. (或 I am carrying a shopping bag which was made by my mom.)

5. He is riding a bike that is very expensive. (或 He is riding a bike which is very expensive.)

6. The man whose voice is very deep answered the phone.

7. The nurse that (或 who) helped us was very patient. (或 The nurse that/who was patient helped us.)

8. We know a lot of people who live in Taidong.

9. Do you know the girl that John is talking to? (Do you know the girl to whom John is talking?)

10. I gave her all the money that I had.

11. Peter's soup, which is in the fridge, is too salty.

12. Your mom, who called this morning, will call again tonight.

12-5-6 英文該怎麼寫？

1. The woman who lives next door to you is my English teacher.

2. Have you found the scooter that you lost?

3. This is the worst movie that I've ever seen.

4. The science-fiction novel that you bought last week is very interesting.

5. This is the air conditioner that my father just bought.

6. My vacation, which is from July 3rd to 6th, is not very long.

7. The cram school where I study is very popular. (The cram school at which I study is very popular.)

8. Due to the energy crisis, everything has become (more) expensive.

9. When I am using the computer, please don't unplug it. (Please don't unplug the computer when I am using it.)

10. My mom doesn't allow me to use plastic bags.

11. The novel that I bought yesterday is very interesting.

12. The shopping bags which were given away by the department store are very big. (或 The shopping bags that the department store gave away are very big.)

第十三課　省略who/whom/that/which 的關係子句

13-5-1 選選看

1. a/b 2. a 　　3. a 　4. a 　5. a
6. a/b 7. a 　　8. a 　9. a 　10. a/b
11. a 12. a 　13. a 　14. a/b 15. a/b
16. a 17. a/b 18. a/b 19. a/b
20. a (關係代名詞前有逗號不可省)

13-5-2 請將兩句併為一句，並將關係代名詞或其後面的 be 動詞省略：

1. Do you know the boy we met yesterday?
2. I don't like the table my parents bought yesterday.
3. The apples laid on the table are sweet.
4. Do you know the girl riding the bike with Tom?
5. Peter, the person we met yesterday, is very nice.
6. I told you about the woman living next door.
7. The bank robbed last week is near my apartment. (或 The bank near my apartment was robbed last week.)
8. Jane's mom, a musician, passed away last night.
9. The temple we visited last night is very old.
10. We went to Seoul, the capital of Korea, last month.

13-5-3 問答

1. She had to pass written and driving tests.
2. It was quite successful.
3. She was going to drive to a supermarket.
4. It is a few blocks from our home.
5. He stopped her to ask her, "Aren't you the person who always makes us ride bikes or take public transportation?" (或 Beeause Mom is the pevson who alway makes them ride bikes or take public transportation.)
6. She said, "I need more practice to master my driving skills."

7. It took her two hours to shop for groceries.

8. She plans to drive to Puli.

9. He took out his mountain bike and said happily, "I guess we can all take our bikes to Puli and ride around that beautiful town."

10. No, he didn't go to Puli with his parents.

11. He has a final exam, (which is) scheduled for the 21st of June.

13-5-4 改錯

1. This is the convenience store which sells cheap sushi. (或 This is the convenience store selling cheap sushi.)

2. The temple I visited last weekend is very old.

3. The day I arrived was very warm.

4. Is he the boy living next door? (或 Is he the boy who lives next door?)

5. Bob, interested in music, decided to become a musician.

6. Ms. Lin, who is very smart, lives on the corner of the street.

7. The man who ate 30 hamburgers in an hour died.

8. He is the man you called last night.

9. She always likes to stay in a hotel where she can swim. (或 She always likes to stay in a hotel in where she can swim.)

10. Summer is the time I go swimming a lot. (或 Summer is the time when I swim a lot. 或 Summer is the time for me to swim a lot.)

13-5-5 英文該怎麼寫？

1. The final exam (which/that) I took this afternoon was very difficult.

2. He doesn't know the reason (why) I stayed at home.

3. Next week I will drive you to Puli, where my grandma lives.

4. The groceries (which/that) my mom bought were very heavy.

5. The supermarket (which is) a few blocks from my home is very big.

6. The air conditioner (which) my parents bought last summer is

broken.

7. The temperature (which) I like is 20 degrees Centigrade.

8. This shopping bag (that) my mom made is very beautiful. (或 This shopping bag (that was) made by my mom is very beautiful.)

9. Mangoes and lychees, which are in season now, are very cheap.

10. That girl wearing a confident smile on her face is our class leader.

第十四課　如果 if...

14-5-1 選選看

1. b   2. c   3. b   4. a   5. c
6. b   7. b   8. a   9. c   10. b
11. c   12. a   13. b   14. c   15. b

14-5-2 填填看

1. had gone to Puli with my parents
2. been
3. were raining
4. come
5. called
6. had read
7. wouldn't
8. took

9. hadn't been
10. hadn't given

14-5-3 問答

1. They came home a week later.

2. It got burnt by the sun and it started peeling. (或 It got burnt by the sun and was as red as a cooked lobster.)

3. She kept nagging him because he hadn't used sunscreen.

4. The writer felt glad that he didn't go with his parents because he might have flunked that important exam.

5. He got a good score on the test.

6. She saw a pile of untouched newspapers lying in the corner of the living room.

7. No, she doesn't. She wishes that he wouldn't just bury his nose in textbooks. (或 No, she wants him not to bury his nose in textbooks.)

8. She wants him to learn about some current events.

9. The guard does it every day.

10. If fewer and fewer people read newspapers, sooner or later,

all newspapers will either go online or disappear altogether.

14-5-4 改錯

1. If I <u>were</u> not an only child, I would not feel so lonely and pressured.
2. Mom <u>would</u> not be happy if I didn't read the newspaper.
3. If I had read the newspaper, Mom <u>wouldn't have been</u> so upset.
4. I wish I <u>could</u> have another cat in addition to Inky.
5. She wishes she <u>had learned</u> English when she was a little girl.
6. If I sell my scooter, I <u>will</u> buy a bike instead. (或 If I <u>sold</u> my scooter, I would buy a bike instead.)
7. If she wants to adopt my cat, I will give it to her.
8. If it rains tomorrow, I will still go hiking.
9. If we <u>go</u> out, Mom will unplug all of the electronic appliances. (或 If we went out, Mom would unplug all of the electronic appliances.)

14-5-5 英文該怎麼寫？

1. If you see him, tell him that I am looking for him.
2. If I had been there at that time, I would have been upset.
3. If I were making money now, I would buy a bicycle.
4. If you had put on sunscreen, your face would not be peeling now.
5. If it doesn't rain tomorrow, I will go to Puli.
6. If I knew her cell phone (或 mobile phone) number, I would call her immediately.
7. If I had had a digital camera at that time, I would have taken a picture of that cat.
8. If you don't bring a shopping bag, you will have to buy plastic bags.
9. If it is not hot and humid, I won't turn on the air conditioner.
10. If he doesn't ride his bicycle, he will take public transportation. (表示他平常的習慣。)

10. If you call her, you ask her to see me this afternoon.

If he didn't ride his bicycle, he would take public transportation. (他現在有騎腳踏車，如果他沒騎的話，他會搭公共交通工具。)

第十五課　雖然……但是，因為……所以

15-5-1 選選看

1. a　2. a　3. c　4. b　5. b
6. a　7. b　8. a　9. a　10. c
11. b　12. a　13. a　14. a　15. b
16. c　17. c　18. a　19. b　20. b

15-5-2 填填看(＊注意：句子第一個字母要用大寫。)

1. even
2. even though
3. Even though
4. even
5. even though
6. even though
7. even though
8. even though
9. Even though
10. Even if
11. even
12. even if
13. even though
14. even
15. Even

15-5-3 問答

1. He saw depressing words like "financial crisis," "recession," and "high unemployment" in the paper.
2. He told him about his father's recent layoff.
3. He might have to drop out of school and take some odd jobs to help them out.
4. Some double-income families are in trouble because of business closures and downsizing.
5. The government distributed consumption coupons.
6. They are to stimulate (或 boost) consumption.
7. No, he receives the same amount of pocket money.
8. Many college graduates are anxious because they can't find jobs.
9. No, he hasn't found a job.
10. He hopes the global financial crisis will be over soon.

15-5-4 改錯

1. My mom never uses the air

conditioner, even <u>though/when</u> it is hot.

2. His high score was <u>because</u> he worked very hard.（或His high score was <u>due to his hard work</u>.）

3. Mom was very upset even <u>though</u> I got a good score.

4. Despite the rain, we enjoyed our trip to Yilan.

5. I didn't go cycling because <u>of</u> the rain.

6. This scooter is not worth <u>buying</u>.

7. <u>Although</u> I see her every day, I've never spoken to her.

8. Our anxiety was <u>due to</u> the high unemployment in Taiwan.

9. <u>Even though</u> I got my own consumption coupons, I gave them to Mom.

10. He isn't depressed even <u>though</u> he was laid off.

11. Despite <u>dropping</u> out of school, he continued studying.（或 <u>Although</u> he dropped out of school, he continued studying.）

12. Many people lost their jobs because <u>of</u> business closures and downsizing.

13. Jie Ming would take some odd jobs even <u>if</u> his parents had jobs.

14. Many restaurants went out of business because <u>of</u> the recession.

15. Thanks to <u>his good advice</u>, I could find a job.

16. My cousin is still job hunting despite <u>even though</u> he graduated from a renowned university.

17. <u>Despite</u> their double income, they can't afford a car.

18. Mom unplugged the electric appliances <u>because</u> she wanted to save energy.

19. No one is buying this book even <u>though</u> it is so interesting.

20. Because he has often helped me, I should help him this time.（或He has often helped me, so I should help him this time.）

15-5-5 英文該怎麼寫？

1. Even if he doesn't come, I will go to a movie.

2. Even though he came, we didn't go to a movie.

3. Even though he worked very

hard, he was laid off.

4. He was laid off because the company didn't have any business.

5. Even though the air conditioner is not expensive, I decided not to buy it.

6. Because he is not interested in current events, he doesn't read newspapers.

7. Because we received consumption coupons, we all went shopping.

8. He doesn't know anything, even about the global financial crisis.

9. Due to the recession, many restaurants have gone out of business.

10. To boost consumption, the government has distributed consumption coupons to every Taiwanese citizen.

11. This lousy movie isn't worth watching.

12. This two-story house is worth buying.

第十六課 你說、我說、他說

16-5-1 選選看

1. c　2. c　3. c　4. b　5. c
6. b　7. c　8. c　9. c　10. c
11. b　12. b　13. b　14. a　15. c
16. c　17. b　18. c　19. b　20. c

16-5-2 填填看（請選最適合的自填入空格中。）

1. interested
2. shocked
3. disappointing
4. excited
5. satisfied
6. depressed
7. annoyed
8. confused
9. interesting
10. amused

16-5-3 問答

1. Jie Ming sent a text message to the writer this morning.

2. Jie Ming's parents got full-time jobs.

3. Jie Ming would like to spend his consumption coupons buying books.

4. The writer asked Jie Ming to meet him at the main entrance to the book fair.

5. He hardly knows anything

about Thailand.

6. A Thai writer (或 novelist) wrote *The Judgment*.

7. Many people lined up for the book signing. (或 They lined up for getting the writer's autograph.)

8. Jie Ming and the writer used to get pop singers' autograph.

9. Yes, he did. He bought the Thai novel, *The Judgment*.

10. No, he doesn't. He doesn't read books only for the sake of passing exams.

16-5-4 改錯

1. He asked her to meet him at the main entrance to the building.

2. I was wondering what kind of books they bought.

3. His mom asked him when he would go to the book fair.

4. She told me that she had watched a great movie the other day.

5. "I just thought of something," he announced, "Tomorrow is my birthday."

6. He whispered to me, "This scooter is not worth buying."

7. I forgot where I bought this novel.

8. He asked her who her favorite novelist was.

9. He said that she was taking a shower now.

10. He wanted to know whether I could go to the book fair with him or not.

11. I finally realized that The Judgment was written by a Thai novelist.

12. He argued that many people lost their jobs because of business downsizing.

13. He told me happily that he had got the novelist's autograph.

14. I was embarrassed because I forgot today was her birthday.

15. The novelist looked exhausted after signing so many books and talking to so many people.

16. We were surprised when thy got married.

17. Her exam score seemed disappointing.

18. She feels bored from doing the same thing every day.

19. Mom told me, "If I were you,

I wouldn't jut bury my nose in textbooks."

20. They were <u>shocked</u> to hear about the earthquake.

16-5-5 英文該怎麼寫？

1. If I hadn't gone to the book fair, I wouldn't have met that Thai novelist.

2. Even if they had gone to the book fair, they wouldn't have gone to the book signing.

3. His mom said, "Now, I know that you don't read just to pass exams." (或 His mom said, "I just realized that you don't study for sake of passing exams.)

4. He asked me if I knew which country was the guest of honor.

5. Many people lined up to get the novelist's autograph.

6. Mom asked me to unplug the electric appliances.

7. Mom was excited when she got her driver's license.

8. This year's book fair was really satisfying.

9. I asked him to find out if the library had today's newspapers. (或 I asked him to find out whether the library had today's newspaper or not.)

10. She told me that the movie she had watched today was very disappointing.

總複習解答

I. 選擇題

1. a 2. b 3. b 4. c 5. b 6. c 7. b 8. b 9. c 10. b
11. c 12. c 13. a 14. a 15. b 16. c 17. c 18. c 19. b 20. a
21. b 22. c 23. c 24. a 25. c 26. c 27. c 28. c 29. c 30. a

II. 填充題

1. spread
2. caught
3. spotted
4. taken
5. debating
6. left
7. anxiously
8. drew
9. surprisingly
10. shown
11. gave
12. foldable
13. laid
14. Challenged/Being challenged
15. lying
16. in
17. on
18. take
19. writing
20. peeling 或 to peel
21. buried
22. to
23. paying
24. with
25. admitted
26. laid
27. dropped
28. electric 或 electrical
29. temperature
30. saving

III. 改錯

1. They got married last Friday.
2. Unlike his wife, he doesn't have a night life. He doesn't like going out at night.

3. I will pick you up（接機）<u>at</u> the airport <u>on</u> Sunday morning.
4. The civil servant whom you met in the office is very friendly.
5. The woman <u>who</u> lives next door to us is a doctor. 或 The woman <u>living</u> next to us is a doctor.
6. Do you know the girl that Jack is dancing <u>with</u>? 或 Do you know the girl <u>with whom</u> Jack is dancing?
7. The museum（博物館）we wanted to visit was closed.
8. Even <u>though</u> he can't drive, he bought a car.
9. She doesn't enjoy the job <u>even though</u> it is high-paying.
10. Although she has a<u>n</u> important job, she isn't well <u>paid</u>.
11. I like searchi<u>ng</u> for information on the Internet. 或 I like <u>to</u> search for information on the Internet.
12. This mountain bike <u>does</u> not belong to me.
13. I <u>am</u> afraid of cockroaches（蟑螂）.
14. She <u>taught</u> me how to play the saxophone.（或 She is teaching me how to play the saxophone.）
15. Not until he had had <u>a</u> toothache for a week <u>did he go</u> to see a dentist.
16. The final exam, which was <u>held</u> on July 1st, was very challengi<u>ng</u>.（也可以省 which was）
17. If I <u>hadn't played</u> computer games, I could have finished my homework on time.
18. I wish I <u>could</u> play tennis.
19. His mom told him <u>not to</u> stay up late（開夜車）playing computer games.
20. I asked her <u>if she had</u> to go now.

IV. 翻譯
1. After graduating from college, I want to get into a graduate school.
2. We subscribe to two newspapers and three magazines.
3. I envy him for having a high-paying job.
4. I bought a dozen energy-saving light bulbs.
5. He has worked for（或 at）this electric appliance store for three years.

6. In order to save energy, he unplugged the air conditioner.

7. I will send you back a text message within three days.

8. Even if I have a headache, I will go to the book fair.

9. Mom told me not to study for the sake of passing tests.

10. The stray cat isn't in the tree, nor is it behind the wall.

11. The woman wearing a striped dress is my Thai teacher. 或 The woman in the red striped dress is my Thai teacher.

12. I'm excited because he gave me a foldable bike as a birthday present.

13. He is disappointed with his English score.

14. Please tell me where the art museum is.

15. Dad suggested that I sell the scooter.

16. In summer, my favorite fruits are mangoes and lychees.(這裡水果不是總稱而是種類，可以加 s。)

17. The Judgment is a book in which you will be interested.

18. I know a girl whose elder sister is your sister-in-law.

19. If I had read the textbook, I might (或 would) have passed the English exam.

20. If I had eaten(或 had) breakfast this morning, I wouldn't have been so hungry in class.

編後語

文庭澍

　　炎炎夏日溽暑伏案寫書時，不時接到讀者來信，聲聲催促下才有這本書的問世。許多讀者從初級本上冊開始，循序漸進，一步步讀完了高級本上冊後，來信中充滿成就感卻難掩心中焦慮：如果讀完六冊《專門替中國人寫的英文課本》並寫畢每課作業後，下一步該怎麼辦？其實這六冊書是綜合我 30 年來教英文所得，點出學生易犯的文法錯誤，詳加說明；然而學習英文之路永無止盡，讀者完成這六本後還可以利用下面延伸閱讀清單，繼續學習，如果其間遇到任何一本書中的問題，隨時歡迎寫信給我 wentingshu@gmail.com。各位的來信豐富我的教學，使我更瞭解學生面臨的問題，及作為一個老師該怎麼用最清楚易解的文字來解答這些問題。以下是我推薦聯經長年以來出版的一些好書，希望讀者持續以克服初、中、高級本六冊的恆心，繼續征服以下一系列的英文好書：

1. 《專門替中國人寫的文法書》、《實用英語文法百科》、《一生必學的英文文法》

　　讀完《專門替中國人寫的英文課本》六冊書後，如果還想對英文文法有通盤性的瞭解，可以先讀李家同教授寫的《專門替中國人寫的文法書》，接著再攻政大陳超明教授的《一生必學的英文文法》，如果想更深入瞭解英文文法，吳炳鍾先生教父級的一系列《實用英語文法百科》，可讓你的文法立於不敗之地。

2. 《全家學英文》、《美國最新口語》、《聽聽美國人怎麼說》

　　學完了以文法為取向的書後，讀者如果想換個口味，學點輕鬆活潑的會話，以《全家學英文》最容易上手，這套書是我和美國籍老師 Kristin Fritzpatrick 合著，包括親子書和兒童書共兩冊，內容以每日一早起床開始、上床睡覺收尾的一天時間內常用的英語句型，有趣而實用。家中有小朋友的父母，還可以利用兒童書伴陪小朋友做英文作業。如果想進一步提升口語能力，建議讀者閱讀懷中寫的《美國最新口語》及黃希敏教授寫的《聽聽美國人怎麼說》。

3.《英語發音百分百》

　　《專門替中國人寫的英文課本》雖附光碟，也在初級本下冊涵蓋英語發音，但這套書並不是有專門教發音的書。讀者如果想糾正自己的英語發音，還是得求助於于宥均老師寫的《英語發音百分百》。于老師點出許多台灣學生英語發音的問題，並用生動的筆調，清楚的圖表，提出解決之道。除了發音外，這本書後面附的數詞與時間等讀法，讓讀者知道如何正確答出數字、地址、日期、數學算式，大大補強《專門替中國人寫的英文課本》數詞部分之不足。

4.《用英文說台灣》、《用英文寫台灣》、《用英文遊台灣》

　　《專門替中國人寫的英文課本》高級本開始有文章出現，如果讀者想瞭解一些與台灣節慶、小吃及生活點滴相關的文章，可讀我和 Cathy Dibello 教授合寫的《用英文說台灣》及黃玟君教授《用英文遊台灣》，如果想提筆寫些與台灣生活有關的短文，就非得讀通黃玟君教授寫的《用英文寫台灣》不可。

5.《讀李家同學英文》

　　李家同教授的散文有的是真人真事，有的純屬虛構，不論真實或虛構，篇篇真誠感人。這些短文經一位中文程度與我們不相上下的美國人 Nick Hawkins 翻譯成英文，再配上周正一先生與譯者所撰寫的詳細解析。讀者可先讀一小段中文部分，心中揣摩英文該怎麼說，再比對 Nick Hawkins 先生的英文翻譯。有心讀這套書的讀者請千萬不要跳過譯者及解析老師書前的導讀。

6. 《好字大——升大學英文救命單字》、《追根救底》

　　許多學生將自己英文不好歸咎於生字背得不夠多，但死記生字並非易事，台灣補教界名師李立崴先生，在眾多生字中找出 1200 個「好字」，讀者若能掌握基本盤的 1200 字，應考時可省力不少。另外一個記生字的方法是瞭解字的字根，也就是字首或字尾，以此類推，不必死背也可以認得好多生字。

7. 《紐約時報英文解析》

　　許多英文學到某個程度的人共同的願望是能讀懂網路上的新聞，但每日新聞包羅萬象，如何在千百條新聞中選擇符合自己需要並進一步讀懂卻非易事，幸好有李志清教授主導的解析團隊，從《紐約時報》中挑出適合國人閱讀的文章，在用字遣詞上加以評註、解析，使學習者可經由專家的「導讀」，一步步享受讀新聞的樂趣。

8. 《英語小冰箱》

　　能開口用英文「秀」自己是許多人的願望，但背了一大堆句子，事到臨頭卻張口結舌，不知如何使用。這本由在韓國教了十多年會話的 Gunther Breaux，教你生活中最新鮮實用的句子，反覆練習，不用冷僻的字眼或艱深的文法，就可以輕鬆「說自己」。

　　以上囊括英文聽、說、讀、寫的英文好書，幾乎都附有光碟，讀者不必花錢進補習班，在家跟著光碟一課課、一本本練習，長此以往，英文一定大有精進，祝各位在英文領域裡更上一層樓。

Linking English

專門替中國人寫的英文課本 高級本下冊

2010年3月初版　　　　　　　　　　　　　　　　　定價：新臺幣280元
有著作權‧翻印必究
Printed in Taiwan.

著　　者　文　庭　澍	
策劃審訂　李　家　同	
發 行 人　林　載　爵	

出　版　者　聯經出版事業股份有限公司	叢書主編　陳　若　慈
地　　　址　台北市忠孝東路四段555號	校　　對　呂　淑　美
編輯部地址　台北市忠孝東路四段561號4樓	林　雅　玲
叢書主編電話　(02)87876242轉226	曾　婷　姬
總　經　銷　聯合發行股份有限公司	封面設計　蔡　婕　岑
發　行　所：台北縣新店市寶橋路235巷6弄6號2樓	
電　　　話：(02)29178022	
台北忠孝門市：台北市忠孝東路四段561號1樓	
電　　　話：(02)27683708	
台北新生門市：台北市新生南路三段94號	
電　　　話：(02)23620308	
台中分公司：台中市健行路321號	
暨門市電話：(04)22371234ext.5	
高雄辦事處：高雄市成功一路363號2樓	
電　　　話：(07)2211234ext.5	
郵政劃撥帳戶第0100559-3號	
郵撥電話：27683708	
印　刷　者　世和印製企業有限公司	

行政院新聞局出版事業登記證局版臺業字第0130號

本書如有缺頁，破損，倒裝請寄回聯經忠孝門市更換。　　ISBN　978-957-08-3562-5 (平裝)
聯經網址：www.linkingbooks.com.tw
電子信箱：linking@udngroup.com

國家圖書館出版品預行編目資料

專門替中國人寫的英文課本 高級本
下冊/文庭澍著．李家同策劃審訂．初版．
臺北市．聯經．2010年3月（民99年）．
224面．19×26公分．（Linking English）
ISBN　978-957-08-3562-5（平裝附光碟）

1.英語　2.讀本

805.18　　　　　　　　　97015241

聯 經 出 版 事 業 公 司

信 用 卡 訂 購 單

信 用 卡 號：□VISA CARD □MASTER CARD □聯合信用卡

訂 購 人 姓 名：＿＿＿＿＿＿＿＿＿＿＿＿＿＿＿＿＿＿

訂 購 日 期：＿＿＿＿＿年＿＿＿＿月＿＿＿＿＿日 （卡片後三碼）

信 用 卡 號：＿＿＿＿ ＿＿＿＿ ＿＿＿＿ ＿＿＿＿ ＿＿＿

信 用 卡 簽 名：＿＿＿＿＿＿＿＿＿＿(與信用卡上簽名同)

信用卡有效期限：＿＿＿＿年＿＿＿＿月

聯 絡 電 話：日(O)：＿＿＿＿＿＿夜(H)：＿＿＿＿＿＿

聯 絡 地 址：□□□＿＿＿＿＿＿＿＿＿＿＿＿＿＿

＿＿＿＿＿＿＿＿＿＿＿＿＿＿＿＿＿＿＿

訂 購 金 額：新台幣＿＿＿＿＿＿＿＿＿＿＿＿＿元整

（訂購金額 500 元以下,請加付掛號郵資 50 元）

資 訊 來 源：□網路 □報紙 □電台 □DM □朋友介紹
□其他＿＿＿＿＿＿＿＿＿＿＿＿＿＿＿

發 票：□二聯式 □三聯式

發 票 抬 頭：＿＿＿＿＿＿＿＿＿＿＿＿＿＿＿＿

統 一 編 號：＿＿＿＿＿＿＿＿＿＿＿＿＿＿＿＿

※ 如收件人或收件地址不同時，請填：

收 件 人 姓 名：＿＿＿＿＿＿＿＿＿＿ □先生 □小姐

收 件 人 地 址：＿＿＿＿＿＿＿＿＿＿＿＿＿＿＿＿

收 件 人 電 話：日(O)＿＿＿＿＿＿夜(H)＿＿＿＿＿＿

※茲訂購下列書種,帳款由本人信用卡帳戶支付

書　　　　　　　名	數量	單價	合　　計
	總　　計		

訂購辦法填妥後

1. 直接傳真 FAX(02)27493734

2. 寄台北市忠孝東路四段 561 號 1 樓

3. 本人親筆簽名並附上卡片後三碼(95 年 8 月 1 日正式實施)

電 話：(02)27683708

聯絡人:王淑蕙小姐(約需 7 個工作天)